TANK ATTACK

He heard it then, a faint clanking sound, off there to the east. The sound grew louder, and now it was joined by the noise of motors.

"They're coming," Andrews called, and settled his cheek against his carbine.

His fire swept the area to the right of the big tank and he saw men go down. He did not count them. He was only vaguely aware of the bodies dropping, to lie sprawling and inert on the snow. He fired until he could see no more men advancing toward him.

Behind him a tank-destroyer was pumping shells at the oncoming tank, but they were bouncing off the thick armor that protected its front.

"Get off to one side, hit them in the side," he muttered savagely. "You'll never get a shell through that armor."

As if his thought were a command, the tank-destroyer lurched off. Then it began firing again.

Its second shell penetrated the tank. Somebody screamed inside the tank, and Gawasowanee saw flame spurt outward through the opening the shell had made. A man tried to climb out of the tank and somebody's bullets caught him in the chest and drove him backward.

The screaming of the Germans grew shriller.

```
ARMCHAIR "FAMILY" BOOKSTORE
   PAPERBACK EXCHANGE—COMICS
OPEN WEEKDAYS 10-9 SAT. 10-6 (SUNDAY CALL)
       3205 S.E. MILWAUKIE AVE.
    PORTLAND, OREGON 97202 (238-6680)
```

We will send you a free catalog on request. Any titles not in your local book store can be purchased by mail. Send the price of the book plus 50¢ shipping charge to Leisure Books, Two Park Avenue, New York, New York 10016. Attention: Premium Sales Department

Titles currently in print are available for industrial and sales promotion at reduced rates. Address inquiries to Nordon Publications, Inc., Two Park Avenue, New York, New York 10016, Attention: Premium Sales Department.

THE BATTERED BASTARDS

GORDON FRENCH

LEISURE BOOKS • NEW YORK CITY

A LEISURE BOOK
Published by

Nordon Publications, Inc.
Two Park Avenue
New York, N.Y. 10016

Copyright © 1979 by Nordon Publications, Inc.

All rights reserved
Printed in the United States

1

The road to Bastogne was cluttered with men, men who were weary with battle, the lines of fatigue etched sharply on their faces. They carried their carbines, their gear, as men might who have looked into the yawning doors of Hell and been saved from entering by some miracle of chance.

Some of them stumbled as they walked and only righted themselves by some sharp jerk of tired muscles. Their eyes were vacant, staring. Weariness was in each one of these men, a weariness that seemed to ooze almost from their very pores.

Alan Bishop walked with head erect, fighting off the tiredness inside him. He wore the stripes of a sergeant and he had been fighting here in Europe for what seemed an eternity. From time to time he glanced behind him, looking at the men who came trailing after him. They were here, the men of his platoon—or what was left of them.

They were moving west from Luxembourg, away from the front line of battle. They had been pulled back out of the fighting for a rest. They were to be quartered at Bastogne for a couple of weeks. There would be no more fighting for them. At least, for a while.

"I want to sleep," Alan told himself. "Dear God, how I want to sleep!"

To sleep, to forget the constant firing of his carbine, to ignore for a while the enemy in front of him, shooting back at him, to kill him. To be able to ignore the threat of big Mark IV tanks rumbling over the ground at him, spitting death from their cannons.

At his heels somebody stumbled and cursed wearily. Alan grinned. That would be Max Gluber swearing in a monotonous undertone. Of them all, Max was the only man who did not want to go to Bastogne.

Max Gluber was a German Jew, a big man heavy with muscle and filled with hatred of Adolf Hitler and all that Hitler stood for. He was a naturalized United States citizen and had been among the first to join the army right after Pearl Harbor, when Germany had declared war on the United States.

Max lived only to kill Germans.

"Maybe I can't get Hitler," he would say. "But I sure as hell can get the men who do what he tells them to."

Max never took prisoners. Ever since they had first dropped into Belgium to begin the assault on Antwerp, Max had been a killer. He snarled when the enemy lifted its arms and shouted out that they were surrendering.

"Not to me," he would mutter, and then his carbine would begin chattering and those Germans would drop where they stood.

Alan never reprimanded him. He understood what made Max so grim. If somebody had been killing his people in gas ovens and torture chambers, if they had been experimenting on them as German doctors had been doing to the Jews, he would have felt the same way. Let Max kill, and kill as many men as he chose to kill.

Max was a damn good soldier. He obeyed orders, he fought with the courage of a cornered lion, and he was always in the forefront of the battle. The only trouble with him was—if one could call it that—he never took a single prisoner.

"They wanted to fight, so let them fight, damn it!

Prisoners don't have to fight. I want them to fight me so I can kill the whole fuckin' bunch of them."

Alan grinned. He turned and called back over his shoulder, "Cheer up, Max. It'll only be a couple of weeks. Then they'll send us back."

"I could kill a lot of Germans in two weeks," Max growled.

"Have a heart, Maxie," called Joe Sullivan from behind him. "I feel like I been in the ring for a hundred rounds. I need a break."

Joe Sullivan was a boxer. A good one, too. If it hadn't been for the war, he might have been fighting for the championship. He brooded now and then on what the war meant to him, talking about the club fights he had been in as a youngster, how he had fought and clawed his way to the top. He was in line for a chance at the champion when the government had sent him those familiar greetings, with an invitation to become a member of Uncle Sam's army.

"Save your breath, paleface," muttered the man behind him, whose hair was red under his helmet.

Joe Sullivan grinned through his mud-streaked face. "Hey, Indian! This ain't like your reservation life, is it?"

Paul Andrews chuckled. A Mohawk Indian, he was the most silent member of the platoon, rarely speaking unless spoken to. He would sit—when he could—on a rest break, fondling his carbine that he always kept polished, ready for instant use. In his native language, he was known as Gawasowanee, Big Snowsnake.

"It's better," the Mohawk growled. "I get to kill palefaces, as many as I feel like, and nobody stops me. It's a good life, Joe."

Joe turned and looked back at him. "That's quite a speech, Paulie."

7

"You keep looking where you're going, paleface. I've never taken a red scalp before."

Joe laughed. He knew that when time permitted, Gawasowanee took German scalps. He had a long knife in his belt, a knife he kept sharp as any razor ever made. When he got the chance, he gripped a dead German's hair, ran his knife around its edge, and lifted off the scalp just as one of his ancestors might have done.

It was against regulations. Or was it? There was nothing in any of the Army manuals that said you could not scalp the enemy.

A platoon had heard word about the scalpings from some of the Germans they had captured (Max Gluber had had no hand in taking these prisoners). They were scared shitless of it and looked in awe on these American fighting men who ripped off the hair of the dead Germans they killed.

Once or twice an officer had come along inquiring about the scalping, but 2 platoon denied any knowledge of it. Oh, the officers had questioned Paul Andrews more than once, they knew he was a Mohawk, but the platoon had closed its ranks against any and all inquiries.

"What the hell's the difference?" Alan Bishop had asked a major once. "The krauts are dead and these scalpings sure grab them where it hurts."

"It's inhuman," the major had sputtered.

"Hell, they're dead. They don't feel a thing." And he had added with a wry grin, "It scares the living hell out of them, too."

The major had agreed with that all right. He had spoken with some of the German prisoners.

"Call it psychological warfare," Alan had added. "That's a big thing right now."

"Just keep it quiet," the major had begged. "Don't

publicize "

After th , nobody bothered 2 platoon about the scalpings. Gawasowanee carried his scalps in his war bag to bring home to show to his people.

Behind the Mohawk, Lou Princezzi marched along like a man in a daze. He did not hear the banter that passed between the fellow members of his platoon. His mind was an ocean away, back in Newark where his Maria waited for his return.

Lou had married his Maria three weeks before he had been called up to the army. Those three weeks had been a honeymoon spent at Niagara Falls. He remembered so much of those three weeks. So much!

It was the one thing that sustained him in the fighting. Some day the war would end, please God, and he could return to his wife. They would set up housekeeping, Lou would go into the construction business with his father and brothers, he would have a fine house and raise a family.

As he stumbled after the Mohawk, his eyes rested only on those muddy feet before him. He felt neither the weight of his pack nor that of the carbine. He was far away in that hotel room in Niagara Falls and Maria was there in her black nightgown, so thin he could see right through it, and she was smiling at him with love and devotion in her eyes.

Up ahead the line of troops of the 101st Airborne Division were falling out, scattering to the side of the road, to sit or lie flat on their backs on the grass. A column of armored half-tracks came clattering down the road, men in dirty uniforms sitting on them and exchanging insults with the resting soldiers.

Alan Bishop moved among his men, eyeing them. Max Gluber had begun to polish his carbine out of long habit, his thick black brows contorted into a scowl.

Beside him Joe Sullivan had lighted a cigarette and was puffing at it steadily.

Lou Princezzi seemed to be sleeping, eyes closed. To one side of him, the Mohawk was sharpening his long knife.

"Isn't much farther," Alan said to no one in particular.

"Any beds in that town, Sarge?" asked Joe Sullivan, removing his helmet to scratch his red hair.

"You can sleep on the ground and like it," Bishop grinned. "What are you expecting, the Waldorf?"

Paul Andrews paused in the sharpening of his knife. "The ground is the best bed. It keeps you from getting soft."

"I could sleep right here," Lou muttered.

"Sleep, sleep," grumbled Max. "Is that all you can think about when there are Germans to kill? *Ach du lieber!* Who is tired?"

"I got me a pretty wife to dream about, Max."

"*Ach,* so. I was forgetting. Say your prayers, Lou. Maybe your God will end the war while we are relaxing in Bastogne. Then you can go home to your Maria."

"If I do, I'll have a party. You're all invited. There'll be spaghetti and lasagna, all you can eat."

"Will somebody shut him up?" growled a voice. "I'm laying here starving."

"Told you not to gobble up your rations," laughed another.

The reply was unprintable and somebody laughed.

Then they were on the move again, shuffling forward through the damp, cold chill of early December. Mists were gathering on the land on all sides so that it seemed as if they were advancing steadily through a vast cloud.

Occasionally they could make out the ruins of a farmhouse, the brick and stone walls of which were still standing, scorched black by fire. Eyes turned toward those ruins and the moving men thought about the homes they had come from, knowing they were standing unharmed and that those inside them were still alive, unharmed by war.

A car came creeping along the road, moving past the marching soldiers. Voices rose from among the men, calling out to the man who rode beside the helmeted driver.

"Hi, General! You battle weary, too?"

"Save us something for dinner when we get there."

"Watch out you don't break down. This walking is for the birds."

General Anthony McAuliffe chuckled and waved a hand as he swept by. These were his troops, these hard-bitten veterans of the 101st, and nobody knew better than he that every man jack of them deserved the rest toward which they were marching.

The car swept on out of sight.

Behind them they could hear the sudden rumble of the big guns, telling all the world that there was a war on and that Bastogne was only to be an interlude of rest before the rest of them were being thrown against the Germans.

"Sherman was right," a man growled. "War sure is hell."

"Walking is hell, that's what's hell."

"Tell 'em, Bill."

"Save your breath," an officer shouted.

The men trudged on, weary to their bones. Their carbines were heavier than they had ever seemed to be and their packs were irritations on their backs. The mist was thicker now and colder, and some of the men began shivering.

Gawasowanee did not mind the walking. He had

always walked, ever since he had been born on the reservation. He had left the reservation when he was about eighteen to go down and live with relatives in New York City where he had gotten a job as a construction worker.

Mohawks had no fear of heights and when a skyscraper was being built, Mohawks were employed for the high work, up there on the girders where the wind always blew and where a single misstep could mean a frightful fall to death. Gawasowanee had been a good worker. He actually liked running around on those narrow iron beams high above the world.

He smiled faintly as he walked. This fighting was child's play compared to the long hours he had spent on those girders. He would have liked to take a batch of Germans up there and watch them cling to those narrow beams. He might even push them off, if he felt mean enough.

His hand touched his war bag that held the scalps he had taken. He would open his uncles' eyes with those scalps. He wondered how long it had been since a Mohawk had scalped an enemy. Too long a time, he knew that.

Lou Princezzi was remembering the way his Maria had looked when she had taken off the nightgown and run around the room naked for him. God! If only he could be with her a few hours, right now.

"Are you randy, Lou?" she had asked, grinning impishly, her breasts bobbling before his eyes. "Hot? How hot are you, my baby?"

He had been damned randy! She had admitted that a couple of hours later in their bed, covered with sweat, but laughing happily. He had been like a bull. And she had loved it.

A lot of the boys worried about their wives, he knew

that. Left alone, to sit night after night without their men, some of them would turn to other men—the 4Fs, probably, who weren't fit to fight but who could probably screw like hell—and then there would come a Dear John letter telling whatever poor bastard that he no longer had a wife to come home to.

Well, good riddance to that sort of woman! Lou agonized a while, wondering if Maria might succumb to some lecher who would come sniffing around her while he was in Europe.

Lou groaned. War sure was hell to take a man away from the woman he loved and who loved him.

Up ahead Alan Bishop was scanning the countryside. He could make out, or so he thought, a lot of buildings forward of their line of march. That must be Bastogne. He didn't know much about Bastogne, but the next few days would probably tell him all he wanted to know about it.

He must see to his men, once they got there, find some place where they could drop and sleep undisturbed. There would be no beds, the beds were for the officers, but he and his men would be satisfied with any spot of level ground where they could flop and sleep.

He heard an officer shouting orders and turned to wave an arm. "2 platoon over here," he bellowed.

He moved out at a walk, guiding the others. The mist was still thick and heavy, but now the buildings began to take shape. He made out a stable of some sort and brought his men toward it.

He saw hay on the wooden floor of the stable and ladders leaning against an upper floor. Max Gluber came up to stand beside him, glancing around him.

"As good a place as any," Max grumbled.

"Better than most, I'd say."

The other man shrugged. It made no difference to him where he laid his body. If he could not be out there killing Germans, what did it matter? He slung his pack off his back and let it drop to the ground.

"Me for an upper berth," Joe Sullivan said, and headed toward a ladder.

"Don't you want to eat?" Alan yelled after him.

"Sure do. After I sleep."

Alan looked around him, wondering if he ought to post a guard. Ah, the hell with that. They were far enough behind the front lines to know that no kraut was going to come in here shooting at them. Besides, there would be guards set up on the perimeter of the town.

He watched the others move into the big stone stables, empty now of horses, and wondered what family had owned this big place. Judging from what he could see, the family had been well-to-do. He wondered where they were, if any of them might still be alive.

Wearily he moved to a pile of hay, dropped his carbine and pack and lay down on the hay. It was soft. He sank into it as though into the arms of a warm-hearted woman. Alan Bishop scowled. Why did he have to think about a woman now?

He knew why. It was because of Mage Thomas. Madge with the golden hair, with the sweet voice and the disturbingly sensual body. He had been going to marry Madge Thomas a long time ago.

His lips quirked into a wry grin. Madge hadn't been content to be the wife of a newspaper man, because a reporter didn't make enough money to suit her. She had her big blue eyes fastened on greater things.

Yet there had been moments. . . .

That night, for instance, when they had gone up to her apartment and she had changed into that slinky black thing under which she had been naked. His lips grew softer, more gentle, as he recalled those hours on her bed, holding her in his arms and pouring out the strength of his body into her, to which she had responded like a sex-starved alleycat.

There had been other nights like that. And days, too, when they had wandered here and there in Chicago, strolling the walks along Lake Michigan, hand in hand. Dining together in some little restaurant, staring into each other's eyes. They had been very much in love. Very much. Yet always Madge had put him off when he wanted to get serious about their love and marry her.

No, Madge had made that clear enough.

A newspaper reporter didn't make enough money to suit her. Madge had dollar signs in her eyes, through which the love he felt she had for him could not break.

"Sarge, you got any orders?"

It was the Mohawk standing before him, his black eyes studying him. Andrews was gung-ho about fighting. He always wanted to be in there for the kill like Max Gluber.

"Go away, Paulie. Go sleep someplace."

The Mohawk had grinned briefly, nodded, and moved away with that catlike walk of his. Never made much sound except when he was fighting. Then every once in a while, he would let go with the Mohawk warwhoop. It was enough to freeze a man's guts. Alan would have hated to be a German when Gawasowanee let loose with that yell.

The Mohawk wandered off to a remote corner of the building, his eyes scanning every cranny where a man might bed down. He chose an area where two walls met, where by propping his back against those stones, he could see right across toward the doorway.

He sat there, carbine across his thighs and dreamed a little of the woodlands he had roamed as a boy, of the streams he had fished, of the game trails he had walked. He would like to go back to those woods someday when the fighting was all over and buy himself a piece of ground—half a dozen acres, say—and build a house on it.

He would have a couple of horses, some cows and pigs. He would make himself a garden and grow juicy vegetables. He had a green thumb, as the white man said. He could grow any damn thing he set his mind to. And a wife, of course. Some nice Mohawk girl who loved the land as he loved it, a good mother for any children they might have.

Gawasowanee dreamed, but he dreamed with his eyes open and intent on that open doorway. Nobody was going to catch him by surprise.

The men of 2 platoon slept like drugged men. Their bones ached, their flesh was worn, their muscles seemed atrophied. They were sick of war for the most part, though Max Gluber trembled in his slumber, still fighting, and Gawasowanee quivered now and then when his dreams were troubled.

To the east where the battle lines were and behind them, other men planned and plotted the deaths of these five men. Not as individuals, no; nobody under the command of the swastika knew who they were, just *what* they were: the enemy.

And the enemy must be broken. They must be annihilated. The Fuehrer had said so, and the Fuehrer must be obeyed. Adolph Hitler had laid down the rule: advance, sweep everything before you, go on to Antwerp and so divide the enemy forces, turn on each one and annihilate it!

The big guns began to talk, thundering out with their leaden hail. The Panzer divisions began to move, slowly at first, then more rapidly as the big Mark IV tanks started to roll westward. All the power of the Fatherland was gathered here between Echternach to the south and Monschau to the north.

Between those points was the German army under Brandenberger, Manteuffel and the Fifth Panzer army, and Dietrich with the Sixth Panzer army. They were poised, ready to spring forward, to throw the crushing weight of men and armor against the tired American lines.

The Americans were not expecting them. It would be a simple matter to push forward in strength, to throw them back, to cause confusion where there was so much confidence, to wrest victory out of what appeared to be defeat.

On his bed of hay, Alan Bishop stirred restlessly. It seemed almost that in his dreams he was hearing the roaring cannonade of distant guns.

2

Christmas was only ten days away.

There was a terrible coldness across this easternmost part of Belgium, with gray, chilling mists crawling along the ground as though it were a living thing seeking something to devour. In the distance the rumble of big guns could be heard, but the men of 2 platoon gave them no thought as they moved toward a company cook who was making flapjacks.

"I could eat a goddamn mule," Joe Sullivan was saying.

"Mule meat's tough," commented the Mohawk.

Joe Sullivan turned in surprise. "You ever eaten any?"

Gawasowanee grinned. "Sure have, when I was a kid. They don't get porterhouse steaks on the reservation, you know."

Alan Bishop came up to them, paused a moment with his head cocked, they looked at him inquiringly.

"What's up, Sarge?" asked Lou Princezzi.

"He's listenin' for Christmas bells," chuckled Joe Sullivan.

"Listen for yourselves, fatheads. Those are big guns sounding." Big 88s—Alan Bishop knew their sound, all right—were mixing in their salvos with shells from mortars and from the launching platforms where rockets soared up into the leaden sky and away toward the enemy.

"What gives?" he asked the air.

"Come on, Sarge. It's no concern of ours. It's too far away."

The sergeant shrugged. Maybe Lou was right. They were here in Bastogne, in a rest area. No need to worry what was happening so many miles away.

Up ahead, a company kitchen had been set up and a cook was casually flipping flapjacks. The men of the 101st Airborne lined up, their plates and cups in their hands. Hot coffee and flapjacks would go good on such a morning, with the cold and the mist making a man feel like a first cousin to Jack Frost.

The Mohawk took his food and moved away, searching out the others of his platoon until he found Max Gluber. He sat down beside him, and began wolfing down the pancakes. When he was done, he swallowed the last of his coffee and turned to his companion.

"Keep your gun clean, Max," he said softly.

He walked away as the big man with the stubble beard stared after him. "What the hell?" he asked softly, and felt the sudden beating of his thumping heart. Could it be?

Impulsively he walked after Paul Andrews and came up behind him in the line for seconds.

"My gun is always clean," he said slowly.

Gawasowanee did not look at him, but said, "My ancestors are whispering to me, Max, the way they did before the first jump we made. We got fighting ahead of us. Bad fighting. Or maybe good fighting." His lips slid into a grim smile. "You'll get to kill more Germans. Me, I'll take a few more scalps."

Max Gluber regarded his redskinned companion in a mixture of hope and doubt. He said, "You're crazy, Paulie. We got the krauts on the run."

"They can always run the other way."

Sergeant Alan Bishop ate slowly, with relish. His appetite was good. It was always good, he thought morosely. If it weren't for the fact that he was in a war, he might damn well put on some weight. Madge was always telling him in the past that he ate too much.

He was worried, too. He didn't like the sounds of those big guns. There were too many of them, and they kept banging away with too much steadiness. It was almost as if they were heralding the start of an offensive.

"Ah, that's shit," he whispered.

He got up to get more flapjacks.

After breakfast they wandered through the town, stopping to stare at an old man working some leather, or at a pretty young girl who was plucking a chicken. They wondered what it must feel like to live here and listen to those shells day after day, night after night.

They were in a rest area. There was nothing to occupy them but a pack of cards that Joe Sullivan had carried from back home. They played poker, squatting in a circle before the big doorway of the barn, not caring much who won or lost, sunk in their own thoughts. It was just something to do, something to help ease the tautness of their war-worn nerves.

A captain wandered by, paused to watch what they were doing. Alan Bishop looked up at him inquiringly. "Heard some big guns going earlier. They're still pounding away."

The captain said, "Not to worry. Not to worry about a thing."

Only when he had gone did Gawasonwanee mutter, "Shows how much he knows."

Max Gluber laid down his cards. "You been hinting all morning, Indian. What's with it?"

"I told you. My ancestors hape been whispering to

me. We're going to catch hell."

Somebody snorted in disgust, but Lou Princezzi asked slowly, "How soon, Paulie?"

"Damn soon. Before Christmas, certainly."

They all looked at him and nobody opened his mouth. The platoon knew by this time that when the Mohawk talked like that, there was something in the air.

"Bad?" asked Joe Sullivan.

Gawasowanee merely nodded.

They slept during the afternoon after chow and lined up for the hot franks and beans somebody had managed to wrangle for their supper. There was a quietness about 2 platoon that the other groups noted and mocked at.

"You guys look like you'd rather be up there in the front lines than here," a man from 4 platoon grinned.

"Can't get enough of fighting, can you?" laughed another.

It was the Mohawk who answered. He said, "Man, you don't know what fighting is yet. But you will—and soon."

4 platoon had heard tales of this Mohawk. They looked at him and wondered, but they kept their mouths shut and their fingers crossed.

Next morning, they began to hear the rumors.

The Germans were launching an all-out offensive. Already they had broken through at Losheim Gap and were threatening the 99th Division. But they were being held up at St. Vith and again at Losheimergraben where the Americans were fighting savagely as they were desperate.

There was no news from Allied Headquarters and somebody guessed that they were as puzzled by what was going on as were the troops themselves. The Germans were pushing westward, that was a fact. But how strongly were they pushing? And—with what?

The krauts didn't have enough men to send into such an all-out offensive. At least, that was the thinking. But as the hours went by and the sound of fighting grew more fierce, the Americans began to realize that Adolf Hitler had found his troops, somewhere.

Lou Princezzi had been worrying about his wife lately. True, she wrote to him regularly, but recently those letters had not been getting through. He had hoped that the mail would catch up to them at Bastogne.

He asked Alan Bishop, "What about it, Sarge? What's the scuttlebutt?"

"Nobody knows for sure, Lou. That's all I can say."

Lou turned away. He might as well sleep. It seemed that he could never get enough sleep, lately. He guessed it was because he was so damned tired.

Max Gluber stayed close to the Mohawk. If anybody could tell when that attack was coming—if it did—the Indian was the man to be near. Those ancestors of his were really something!

Gawasowanee was cleaning his rifle, making certain that it was in A-1 condition. A paratrooper needed his carbine, it was like an extra arm. Without it he was defenseless.

He looked up as Max squatted beside him. "Another day or two, the way I figure it," he murmured softly. "Then all hell will break loose."

Max smiled faintly. "Good. I'll be ready."

2 platoon woke next morning to the news that a lot of Junkers cargo planes had gone flying overhead during the night filled with kraut paratroopers. They were landing at Malmedy and were apparently on their way to the Meuse River.

The Germans were also murdering prisoners. One hundred and twenty-five men had been machine-gunned down at the Baugnez crossroads. Another German officer had murdered eight Americans by putting the muzzle of his automatic into their mouths and shooting. There were other such reports told by officers who had heard of them with sorrow, bitterness and a furious, deep anger....

Max Gluber nodded heavily when he was told such stories. "It is like the Germans. They have no understanding of humanity. How can you expect it of people who keep the gas ovens going at places like Dachau and Belsen, killing Jews?"

The Mohawk who was sitting nearby smiled faintly. "The Americans keep us Indians on reservations."

Gluber nodded heavily. "It is an example, *ja*. But they do not kill them, they do not massacre them, young and old, nor do they perform operations on them without ether or any other gas to deaden the pain."

He scowled blackly. "They have buried pregnant women in the ground up to their necks when it was time for them to give birth." He spat. "Then ask me why it is I take no prisoners."

Joe Sullivan growled, "I never hated Germans before. But I do now. I'm with Max. No more prisoners for me either."

Alan Bishop was thinking that you couldn't blame an entire race of people for what a few did. Or could you? Was it a poison in the Nazis that made them into such inhuman killers? His hand caressed his carbine. When they came toward Bastogne, as they would, he did not think he would take any prisoners either.

Of course, he might not get the chance.

Lou Princczzi muttered, "If we're to be rested, why haven't orders come for us to pull back, out of Bastogne?"

Alan glanced toward the boy from Newark. "Because

nobody believed the krauts were able to make such an attack. They're going all out, trying to cut a wedge between Montgomery to the north and Patton in the south."

"With us in the middle," nodded Joe Sullivan.

Lou Princezzi was frowning. "How can we hold them? All we have here is the 101st."

Max growled heavily, "We'll hold them with our dead bodies."

Lou sighed. "That's what I'm afraid of."

General Hassen von Manteuffel was in command of the Fifth Panzer Army. He hurled its tanks and soldiers forward toward Bastogne, with every intention of sweeping through it, of killing its defenders, of solidifying his columns and moving them forward through Belgium toward Antwerp.

The attack was begun from Wiltz to the southeast, and from Clervaux to the northeast. His army would smash forward, overrun Bastogne and whatever troops were in it, and then hurl itself westward.

There was a large, flat plain east of Bastogne. It was perfect ground over which to move tanks and troops. Who was there to stop them? And—with what?

Moving into Bastogne on that cold, misty morning were elements of the 9th Armored Division which had tried to hold a roadblock against the surging Germans. Joining them was Combat Command B of the 10th Armored.

Moving out of Bastogne, to the eastward, was 2 platoon, with other elements of the 101st Airborne. The word was that they were to make a stand against the krauts, that they were to keep them away just as long as they could shoot.

They marched through the cold, chilly mists, shoulders hunched and carbines at the ready. They were tired men. They had fought long in this goddamn war and they needed the rest they were never going to get. They did not think; they blanked out all thought, they were automatons being sent out to kill Germans in the hope that if they killed enough of them they would blunt this attack on Bastogne.

They were a part of Team Desobry sent to hold Noville, which was in the direct path of the Second Panzer Division.

To their south, to the west, the Germans were overrunning all the American positions. On the Schnee Eifel an entire regiment had surrendered, after being cut to pieces by tanks and heavy guns. Eight thousand Americans were taken prisoner. At Stoumont a battalion with its tanks were fleeing, but halted long enough to smash some big German Tiger tanks, together with some of their Panthers.

Encouraged by this success, the men of the 30th Division Battalion surged forward and dug in to hold their ground. . . .

At Noville, Alan Bishop lay bellydown on the hard ground. The mists were all around him, gray and cold and wet, and he shivered more than once as he held fast to his carbine. Behind him and his platoon, were a couple of Sherman tanks, reinforced by three tank-destroyers.

"If only the goddamn fog would lift," he muttered.

Joe Sullivan was to his left. He said softly, "A buck I get off the first shot."

"You're on, Joe. But—make it count."

Their eyes strained to see through the fog that was everywhere. It was cold, clammy, and it seemed to their imaginations that out of it would loom the German tanks and the soldiers of the Second Panzer Division. Yet nothing happened. It was quiet. Too quiet.

Paul Andrews lay to one side of his fellows. His black eyes scanned the gray mists, his ears strained for the slightest sound, just as one of his ancestors might have waited in the fogs of New York when it was Mohawk land for an enemy to appear.

He heard it then, a faint clanking sound, off there to the east. The sound grew louder and now it was joined by the noise of motors.

"They're coming," he called, and settled his cheek against his carbine.

The huge Tiger tank loomed up a hundred yards away. Gawasowanee held his fire. His bullets would only bounce off those heavily protected tank walls.

Then he saw the figures moving beside it and behind it, enemy soldiers clad in white as camouflage against the snow and the mists. It was hard to see them at such a distance. Better to let them come a little closer, just a little closer.

He heard Lou Princezzi mutter, "Here they come!"

His carbine jumped as he pulled the trigger. His fire swept the area to the right of that big tank and he saw men go down. He did not count them. He was only vaguely aware of the bodies dropping, to lie sprawled and inert on the snow. He fired until he could see no more men advancing toward him.

Behind him a tank-destroyer was pumping shells at the oncoming tank, but they were bouncing off the thick armor that protected its front.

"Get off to one side, hit them in the side," he muttered savagely. "You'll never get a shell through that armor."

As if his thought were a command, the tank-destroyer lurched of. Then it began firing again.

Its second shell penetrated the tank. Somebody screamed inside the tank and Gawasowanee saw flame spurt outward through the opening the shell had made. A man tried to climb out of the tank and somebody's bullets caught him in the chest and drove him backward.

The screaming of the Germans grew shriller.

Max Gluber smiled grimly at hearing those screams. Inside him there was peace and a great contentment. This was where he should be, firing rounds of death at those oncoming Germans, at the men who had raised Adolf Hitler to the pinnacle of power.

They wanted Hitler, did they? Then let them take what was coming to Hitler and to the Germans who adored him so much!

He began firing slowly, aiming carefully at the troops he could make out in those mists. It occurred to Max that if he found it hard to see those krauts, they were finding it just as difficult to see the men of 2 platoon, bellied down on the ground and behind hillocks. All the Germans could see were the carbine muzzles and the red hail of bullets they were spraying at them.

It gave him an almost orgasmic pleasure to kill Germans. These were the people who delighted in killing Jews. It was the Germans who had built such places as Dachau, Belsen, and Buchenwald. They should be made to pay for those atrocities. He would make them pay and pay and pay. . . .

Lou Princezzi had no emotion in him at all. He was here to kill Germans so as to end the war. With the end of the war, he could go home to his Maria. He felt very cold-blooded, almost as though he were killing insects.

Kill enough of the krauts and they would have to surrender because there would not be enough of them left to wage this war. Kill enough Germans and he would soon be back with his wife.

The white-clad Germans loomed up in the mists almost like targets at a shooting gallery. Didn't the damn fools know they were facing gunfire? They came on at a slow trot and sometimes Lou wondered if they ever thought at all, or were just automatons obeying orders.

Advance, the German High Command had ordered. And advance the Germans did, into the face of the withering gunfire that the Americans were pouring into them.

But now the other tanks were coming up and their cannon and machine-gun muzzles were raking the ground, seeking out the Americans opposing them.

Joe Sullivan hugged the dirt when a shell burst some distance away. He could hear the whine and shrill scream of the shrapnel as it flew through the air and kept his head low, waiting at any second for that hot metal to plow into his flesh. After a time, he realized that he had not been hit.

"Bastards," he whispered, and fired at several men he saw moving toward him. The men went down, lay still.

He saw more men coming toward him through the mists, and these he also shot down, until it seemed to him that he was the only man between the krauts and whatever it was that they wanted, coming so steadily this way.

He did not know how the rest of the fight was going, though he heard Sergeant Bishop firing off to his left and the Mohawk out there to his right, letting off a warwhoop every once in a while.

Joe grinned, imagining what those krauts must think when they heard that blood-curdling cry rising out of the mists. He hoped it scared them shitless.

Sergeant Alan Bishop was praying. He was not a praying man, but now he was remembering a prayer his mother had taught him when he had been a child, and so he whispered that prayer over and over again, even as he fired off his rounds at those ghostly figures moving toward him.

It was too much to ask them to stand up to those tanks. Even when the tank-destroyers scored a hit, the others behind the burning tank came on, clanking and puffing, sliding over the snow as though nothing could stop them.

He felt colder, wetter, and it dawned on him that those mists might be friendly after all. If the Americans couldn't see the Germans, he was damn well certain that the krauts could not see them.

So if the enemy didn't know what it was they might be stepping into, they might hold off and wait for clearer weather. The thing to do was to encourage that sort of thinking by pumping all the shells they could into their ranks.

He glanced left and right. His platoon was holding its own, along with all the rest of the men here at Noville. The question was: what was going to happen when the fog lifted?

As the fog worsened, the firing became sporadic and then stopped entirely. What was the sense of firing at the gray clouds that surrounded them? Nobody could see an enemy, sometimes not even a friend, in this thick muck. The best thing to do was grab a little shuteye so as to be ready for the morning, when—hopefully—the sun would burn away that heavy grayness.

Alan Bishop slept on his carbine, tightly clutching it. So did Joe Sullivan and Lou Princezzi.

Only Max Gluber and Gawasowanee were awake.

The Mohawk edged closer to the other. "Max, I'm going out there to get me a scalp or two."

Max stared at his Indian friend in something like shock. "Are you crazy? There are thousands of them!

They will shoot you full of holes!"

"They won't see me—or hear me."

Max pondered. Something inside him whispered that, since he wanted to kill Germans, it might be a good idea to go along with this crazy redskin. He nodded shortly, getting a firmer grip on his carbine.

"All right. I'm with you."

They began crawling across the frozen ground.

3

It was like crawling through a cloud.

There was nothing to see for more than a yard in front of them. Everywhere the fog was like cotton candy. They moved at a snail's pace, inching forward with their elbows, their bellies close to the cold ground. Out of the corners of his eyes, Max Gluber saw that the Mohawk had his long knife, his scalping knife, between his strong white teeth like a pirate.

Max shivered. If it were not for the fact that the Mohawk was out to scalp Nazis, he might have made some sort of protest. Depriving a man of his hair seemed a silly thing to do, to his mind. Still, it had been a custom of the American Indians when they fought with their enemies and who was he to go against tradition?

He smiled coldly. Scalping was too damn good for those Nazi butchers. He thought about how they had killed so many Jews in their gas ovens and torture chambers and began to wish that he knew how to scalp men, too.

Gawasowanee was sliding forward, always moving. Yet he was quiet, he made no more noise than did the mists as they crept on tiny feet across the land. His knife-blade was cold in his mouth and he made certain that he kept the sharp edge outward lest he cut himself.

Up ahead of them, there were Germans. Somewhere

soon now he ought to be running into one or two of them. He grew more wary, pausing often to listen.

He was upon the man almost before he realized it. Suddenly the German was there, lying motionless, his chin propped on his crossed forearms. Gawasowanee felt his heart leap in excitement and he came close to betraying himself by stabbing outward with the long-bladed knife in his hand.

Then he ralized the German was asleep.

The Mohawk slid closer. He held his knife in his hand, the sharp side upward. One quick movement with that knife, there under the chinstrap of his helmet, and the German kraut was dead.

He stabbed.

His knife's edge went across the throat of the sleeping man so swiftly that the man died before he knew he was being attacked. Blood gushed out and Gawasowanee waited, scarcely breathing.

Only when the kraut slumped in death did he move, cutting through the chin-strap of the helmet and lifting it off so gently he did not make a sound.

He clasped the thick yellow hair of the German and put his knife-edge to it. Gently he cut, slicing into the skin, all around the head. Then, with a swift motion of his hand, he yanked off the scalp.

Max Gluber watched him intently, knowing a grim satisfaction inside himself. Something like this served the Germans right! They had tortured, they had killed. Now it was their turn to be treated with an almost inhuman attitude.

And yet . . . . and yet . . . .

What Paul Andrews was doing was only what his ancestors had done when they took the war trail. A scalp to the Mohawk was only an indication that he had met the enemy and killed him. It was proof of his bravery, of his cleverness in battle.

He waited as Paul Andrews stuffed the scalp back into his jacket pocket. Then Paul turned his head and looked at him, eyebrows raised.

"One more?" he whispered.

Max Gluber felt anxiety come up alive, deep inside him. What sort of damn fool was he to be risking his neck here on the outskirts of the German lines? He might have felt differently if he were the one doing the killing, he knew, but this standing by, as though helpless, was something he did not relish.

To his amazement, he found himself nodding.

What the hell? What difference did it make who killed the krauts as long as they were killed? He tightened his hands on his carbine and began to slide forward beside his companion.

They moved another dozen feet.

The fog was thick about them, they could not see each other. At least, thought Max, nobody could see them either. Maybe Paulie had the right idea, trying something like this in such a mist.

Another German loomed up, crouched on the ground. Max watched Andrews slide closer, saw the dart of his knife, watched as the blood gushed out. Again the helmet came off and the knife made its circle about the scalp.

Gawasowanee ripped off the scalp. It made a faint, tugging sound.

"What is that?" a voice called out of the mists, in German.

Max grinned. "I sneezed," he answered in the same language.

"Be careful, there. Nobody knows where those damned Amerikaners are."

Gawasowanee winked at Max, pushing his face close

to him, then jerked his head. It was time they got the hell out of here.

They slid backward, then turned and began their crawl toward the American lines. It seemed to Max that it was much longer than they had traveled coming here. He was letting the Indian lead the way, but maybe Paul Andrews had lost his direction in the thickness of the mists.

He was about to speak when the Mohawk held up a hand.

An instant later, he was whispering, "Right back where we started from, Max. See? There's your spot, right over there."

Max Gluber blinked. The Indian was right. That was his foxhole, only a yard or two away. With a grunt of thankfulness, he moved into it. Maybe he could snatch a little shuteye now. Tomorrow was going to be hell.

He fell asleep like a tired child.

Dawn was little more than a lightening of the darkness. The mists were still as thick, surrounding everything. Nobody could see anything. But 2 platoon knew the Germans were out there, just waiting for the weak December sun to burn away some of that fog.

Lou Princezzi was hungry. No, worse than that: he was starving. And all he could do was lie here and remember the heaps of spaghetti his mother had made for him, and the lasagna and the sausages with salad. His lips tightened against the saliva gathering in his mouth.

What he wouldn't give to be back in his mother's house, about to dig into a plate of spaghetti! With Maria beside him, of course.

Maria didn't eat as much as he did. She always said she had to keep her figure. Lou spawned a dreaming smile on his mouth. And what a figure! Breasts like cantaloupes, hips like a Grecian lyre, legs like those of Betty Grable. She was a beauty, was his Maria.

His loins began to ache. If only he could have Maria with him in a bed for a few hours!

He chuckled. He didn't want much. An hour and a half to eat one of his mother's meals, and then a couple more hours with Maria in a bed. Talk about Heaven! A man couldn't ask for anything more than that.

Joe Sullivan brooded out at the mist-covered fields in front of him. He was not seeing those fields, or the mists either. He was back in the ring against Benny Sigismundi, exchanging blows. Hey! That had been a fight, that one between him and Benny. They had gone at each other like a couple of mad dogs.

By the eighth round, neither of them could do more than tap the other, they were so exhausted. They had been throwing leather ever since the bell had sounded. His own arms had been so heavy, he could hardly get them up to block the blows that Benny was slamming into him.

He wondered where Benny was getting all that pep. By rights, Benny ought to be as tired as he was himself. He backed up, covering himself, and then it seemed that energy was flooding into his body.

He tried a left hand, another left. Benny backed up. Hey! Maybe he could still win this fight. He drove in, pumping both gloves into Benny, down there in the midsection. Benny wore a puzzled look now, as though he had stepped into a buzzsaw. He lopped a right at him, an overhand swing, one that Benny had ducked all night.

Only Benny didn't duck fast enough this time, probably because he was so tired. His glove had landed flush on Benny's jaw and Benny had gone down. . . .

Something exploded not far away.

Joe Sullivan jerked himself back to reality. That had been an 88 shell. He poked his rifle forward and strained his eyes to see through the fog. The Germans were waking up and getting ready to move forward.

Slowly the minutes oozed along. Even more slowly, the mists began to clear.

As they did, something like horror struck the men of 2 and all the other platoons stationed here. The field before them was covered with German tanks and their motors were starting to rumble to life. Jesus God! Flesh and blood couldn't stand before all that metal!

Sergeant Alan Bishop bit his lip. His eyes went up and down the foxholes that were here. Those tanks would run right over his men. The two tank-destroyers they'd had had been smashed. They had nothing with which to stop the krauts.

"Fall back. Pass the word. Move back," he called.

He began to inch backwards until he felt that what was left of the mists would hide him. Then he stood up and waited, watching as the men on all sides of him came crawling through the fog to join him.

He had no way of knowing what the other troops were doing. The trouble with a battle like this—to the men who were out there in the front lines fighting it, at any rate—was that they had little knowledge of how the fight was going. Only the Brass knew that, and sometimes they didn't know because of a lack of communications.

Alan Bishop felt responsible for his platoon. He had fought with these men ever since the first drop, back there near Arnheim. They had been through a lot of fighting since then. If he was able to, he wanted to keep them alive to go on fighting.

One by one, they joined him, together with other elements of the troops who had been here in this perimeter.

Max Gluber growled, "What now, Sarge?"

"We fall back."

Joe Sullivan was looking at the tanks. "Makes sense. We can't fight those babies, not without bazookas and maybe a tank-destroyer or two."

Paul Andrews said, "Let's make tracks."

His Mohawk blood could understand a pullback. That was the Indian way of fighting. A swift attack, a savage fight, and then fade away back into the forests. Except that there were no forests here.

A man from the 10th Armored team came running up. "Pull back," he panted. "The krauts are in overwhelming force and the order is to save what we can."

Alan Bishop grunted, then waved an arm. "Pass the word. We're going back to Bastogne. And keep together."

Gawasowanee led the way, moving in that slightly pigeon-toed walk he had. His eyes went from left to right. He looked behind him, scanning the ground. In the background he could make out the German tanks moving forward swiftly looking for Americans to kill.

Max Gluber brought up the rear, walking with his head turned so he could see those Germans all the time. It went against him to retreat, but his sound common sense told him that to stay here would mean either death or capture. And if either of those things were to happen, how could he go on killing krauts?

He muttered and mumbled under his breath, but he kept walking. Yet at every step he took, his carbine was in his hands, ready for firing.

Lou Princezzi was sick of this damn war. He had done more fighting in the months he had been here on the European mainland than he had believed possible. He had killed an uncounted amount of Germans and now it seemed he was going to have to kill a lot more—if he lived.

He heard the rumble of guns behind him, the high-screaming of the shells, the muffled *cruuump cruuump* as they landed. A man walking beside him—Lou didn't know where he had come from—said that the Germans had captured an entire hospital unit.

"Saw the whole thing, before I decided it was too hot a place to stay," the man added.

"Jeez, that's bad. If anything happens to those wounded. . . ."

"The krauts'll shoot 'em. You heard what happened in Malmedy when they killed more than a hundred prisoners? Just machine-gunned the lot of them."

"I'm beginning to understand how Max feels about them," Lou muttered. "I'm getting the same kind of hate in me that he has."

If it weren't for the damned krauts, he could be back in Newark with Maria. As he slogged along, he remembered the way she had looked the morning after their first night as husband and wife.

He had awakened to the feel of her warm, naked body beside him under the covers, her touseled black hair on the pillow. She had been awake, had been lying there looking at him, her full lips smiling faintly.

"Hello, husband," she had whispered, and leaned to kiss him.

He could still feel the warm bulges of her breasts against his chest where she had leaned to him as his arms went around her. He remembered the way in which her nipples stood up and nudged him.

Then he had—

Something loomed up to the left, and for an instant, Lou Princezzi was caught off guard. He was staring at a German soldier in those white coveralls they all wore for this winter campaigning.

His hands had acted faster than his brain. They held the carbine at his hip and they didn't bother lifting it or aiming it. His left hand guided the barrel as his trigger finger went into action.

His fire almost cut the kraut in half.

Then he was yelling, "Get them. Get the goddamn bastards!"

All around him men were firing, cursing, running. Lou went with them, seeing the white-clad forms dropping as the accurate rifle fire mowed them down. There was no time for thought. You saw the enemy, you recognized that it was you or him, and you shot—and you shot to kill.

Alan Bishop was trying to bring order out of chaos, seeking to keep his men together. At the same time he understood that it was every man for himself here on the perimeter of the defense forces with the enemy pressing against them, trying to brush them out of the way, to kill them and so clear a path for the advance onward to wherever it was the Germans wanted to go.

Everything had happened so suddenly—with those white forms shaping up out of what was left of the mists—that nobody had any time for thinking. It was fight for your life and hope that everybody stayed alive.

He gunned down two men, watched them drop even as he tensed to fight off another attack. But that attack never came. Suddenly it was quiet, all along this stretch of ground.

Max gluber was snarling. "That's all there was, just a patrol."

"Be grateful, Max," grinned Alan Bishop. "Now let's get a move on. The road is somewhere around here. All we got to do is find it."

They did not know just where they were, but Alan

figured if they went south, they would have to cut across one of the roads leading into Bastogne. That was the focal point. The general was in Bastogne, like a spider in its lair, keeping a weather eye out for everything and everyone around him.

The men trudged on.

Somebody was catching hell back there where they had come from, or maybe it was just the krauts trying to make sure. No matter. If they kept on, they would get to Bastogne and then Alan would be able to report to a superior officer. That was what he wanted to do most, make his report and then flop down somewhere and sleep.

He wondered if he would be allowed to sleep.

They walked steadily, their weapons at the ready. If another German patrol were to run into them, they would not be caught by surprise this time.

Joe Sullivan was thinking of beer. His throat was dry. He ached in his every bone. He was not hungry, but God, he was so damned thirsty! All he could think of was a cold stein of beer. Just one. Was that too much to ask?

I'll pray, he thought. I'll pray that somewhere out here there is a cold beer—just for me.

He began to pray and then he laughed. Imagine praying for a beer when he might be dead the next moment! What damned fools we human beings are.

Instead of everybody getting together and maybe making a big beer-drinking contest out of this goddamn war, men had to go and kill each other. Hey, now. That was quite an idea. Why hadn't somebody thought of it before? Get all the generals together, all the privates, sit them down and serve them beer.

The team that drank the most beer got the—

What? What was it they got? What the hell were they

fighting about anyhow? Joe tried to think, but all he could do was dream of beer.

"Hey, Sarge," he called. "What's this war about anyhow?"

"We got to stop Hitler, Joe. He's a maniac."

"What's he want? What's so fuckin' important to him that we got to be out here in this cold, shooting people?"

"He kills the Jews," Max Gluber said heavily. "They are not Aryans. Hitler thinks Aryans are the superior race. I'm not an Aryan. Neither is Paulie Andrews. He's a Mohawk. Maybe they'd put Indians in their concentration camps, too."

"I would like to scalp Hitler," said Gawasowanee, off to one side. "What a scalp that would be to show my uncles and my cousins."

He began to laugh.

His laughter froze on his lips as he crouched. There was something out there in the mists. His carbine came up and his finger curled about the trigger.

"Hold it, Paulie," Alan whispered.

It was no German out there, it was too small. Besides, it had long yellow hair, whatever it was. Gawasowanee nodded and loped forward.

He saw it was a girl—a girl about fourteen years old, in a ragged scrap of a dress that showed off her legs, with long golden hair falling almost to her hips. Her eyes were very big as he came up to her.

"Hey, sister," he grinned. "You're off limits. What are you doing away out here?"

The girl merely stared at him. Then her mouth trembled into a smile and she began to talk. It was as though a dam had burst in her.

"Hold up, honey," the Mohawk protested. "I can't talk your lingo."

The girl nodded. She was Belgian, he was a Mohawk American. Her blue eyes studied him, then she smiled and said, "Me—friend."

Gawasowanee grinned. "You bet. We're your friends and you're our friend. What are you doing here?"

The others came up to them then and a man from the 705th Tank Destroyer Battalion began to talk to the girl in French. When he was done, he turned to the Mohawk.

"She got separated from her family that fled from the Germans. She is cold and hungry. She wants to know if she can go with you."

Paul Andress grinned and fished in his pocket where there was a broken bit of chocolate he had been saving for emergencies. He handed it over to the girl.

"Tell her we'll feast her in Bastogne, but that she can eat this for now."

Somebody said, "What can we do with a girl?"

Gawasowanee growled, and there was a savage glint in his black eyes. "She goes with us. I'll take care of her."

Her name was Michelle Kubek. Her blue eyes went here and there, somewhat awed at the sight of so many big men. She pressed closer to the Mohawk, who gave her thin shoulder a squeeze.

Then 2 platoon learned that they had stepped into the path of the 705th Tank Destroyer Battalion, which was on its way to reinforce Noville.

"There's a lot of tanks in front of Noville," Alan told a captain.

"We eat tanks," grinned the captain.

As they moved back the way they had come, 2 platoon began to learn something of the magnitude of the German attack.

"They're coming at us in waves," the captain told Alan Bishop. "It caught us by surprise a couple of days ago. We weren't expecting any such big-scale attack. At first the Brass didn't know what to do, but now they've sort of ironed things out."

Bastogne must be held at all costs. The city sat astride the best roads to the west and unless it could be taken by the Germans, it would be like a massive roadblock to their plans.

Of course, they could bypass it, but they would lose time, and *time* was of the essence to Hitler and his dream of winning this war by one smashing blow.

"When we regroup, when Montgomery up north joins in and Patton with his Third Army comes up from the south, we'll crack those krauts the way you crack a louse with your fingernails."

If we're alive, Alan Bishop thought.

4

They came into Noville in the early morning when the Second Panzer Division was mounting an all-out attack, supported by heavy artillery fire. The sound of that cannonading was deafening, the fire-red explosion of the shells, the return fire of the Americans, was like a corner of Hell ripped loose and set free upon the earth.

Into that inferno came 2 platoon, running and dropping, rising to run forward again, seeking out the enemy and not finding them, but digging holes in which to crouch and wait. They lay glaring to the east, out of which the attack would come, and as they lay, they called to one another, repeating the latest news.

Noville had fought and held, but their tank-destroyers had run out of armor-piercing ammo. Now that they had been reinforced by the 705th, they had the shells they needed. Morale was high. No one was dismayed. They were in a fight, but hell! That was why they were here in the first place.

Lou Princezzi was mad. It was all the fault of these goddamn Germans that he wasn't back home with Maria. He could hardly even think of her any more without the Germans showing up to shoot at. Shooting at Germans disturbed his dreams of his wife.

So he crouched now in the wet hole he had dug, his carbine at the ready, and he waited for those white-clad forms at which to shoot. They would not come for a time. They never did until after the artillery barrages had been laid down and then they came following the big tanks, almost like ghosts.

He stared off across the snow-dappled ground, but he was back there at Niagara Falls with Maria naked beside him, her nipples digging into his flesh, her wet mouth open on his own and her tongue slithering over his.

He had caressed her buttocks, slowly and hungrily, reveling in their softness. His hands had urged her loins closer to his, so that she might feel the power of his manhood pressing against her belly.

There had been a fire in his Maria. There had been no shyness about her. She had teased and laughed at him, making ribald comments about his hard-on, asking him what he was going to do with it, now it had grown so big.

Lou Princezzi smiled dreamily. He remembered what he had told her when she had said that. "I'm going to sink it in you, my darling. All the way. You were made for it, or maybe it was made for you."

She had giggled when he'd said that and let her legs widen a little so that he could slip between them. He was on his back, she was on top of him, and—

Tanks were moving toward him. He could see them easily enough now and he could make out, behind them, the shapes of the German infantrymen as they came walking along.

Behind him a tank-destroyer fired.

A tank exploded, bursting into flames. Lou could hear the men inside it screaming for a little while before their voices died away. Lou felt pity for the men, for a moment, before he realized that these men were there to kill him if they could.

He moved his carbine out and began firing at those white-clad figures behind it. He watched them go down without any emotion. It was almost as though he were firing at targets at a penny arcade. As he fired, between bursts he could hear a deep voice muttering something in German.

Ah, that would be Maxie.

How he hated those krauts!

Well, he didn't blame him. If he'd lost his family the way Maxie had, he might do some cursing himself. He saw other krauts begin to fall where Max Gluber was shooting and he knew that if anyone was going to hold up his end of this dirty business, it would be Maxie.

Max Gluber was growling to himself as he fired steadily. That one was for Cousin Helen, that one over yonder near the dead tree was for Uncle Herman. Ah, another for Aunt Gilda, and one for Cousin Wilhelm. He fired steadily, in little bursts, pausing to observe the effect of his bullets.

Not far away Gawasowanee was also throwing his bullets across the land, just as surely and as readily as Max Gluber. The Mohawk fought with emotion strong inside him. There were times when he relived the old days when with a warwhoop and an uplifted tomahawk he might have raced to meet these men and brain them, one after the other.

Sobbing intruded on his thoughts and then he felt a warm body pressing close. He risked a glance out of the corners of his eyes at the girl who lay so tightly against him. She was a thin little thing, but there were curves to her body, too. His eyes had noted them in the thin dress she wore.

Jeez! In this winter weather, she must be damned close to freezing. For a moment Paul Andrews thought of taking off his own jacket to put around her, but there was no time for such niceties at the moment.

The krauts were still coming and he had bullets yet unfired. He began to shoot again, carefully and with a distinct feeling of hatred rising inside him. Those damned krauts were the cause of Michelle's shivering. The poor kid was scared witless. Paulie did not blame her. He would have been scared, too, if he had any sense.

Alan Bishop was worried. He knew that the Germans were too strong for them. They were throwing everything they had at this defense position. Heavy shells, big tanks, soldiers that kept coming no matter how many he and his men dropped. How many more troops did Hitler have anyhow?

He and his men could not hold these positions. The tanks were coming right at them. If they didn't fall back pretty soon, 2 platoon would be dead as doorknobs.

"Let's get the hell out of here," he yelled.

He came to his feet, running, pausing to send back bursts from his carbine at those ghostly German bodies. On all sides of him, men were springing to their feet and moving off to one side, away from that main thrust.

Noville could not stand against all the hardware the krauts were throwing at it. Flesh and blood couldn't take this steady pounding, pounding, pounding. Those huge Mark IV tanks were lumbering forward, firing as they came, and they didn't have enough tank-destroyers to stop them.

The situation was critical.

The men in the front lines, the men at whom the Mark IV tanks were hurling all those shells, knew this. They were battle-hardened veterans, they could tell the way a battle was shaping up. Behind them, the men at headquarters were getting much the same impression.

It was all but impossible to hold Noville against those repeated thrusts of the Second Panzer Division. At the same time it was just about equally impossible to save the men entrenched at Noville.

To add to their firepower, the Third Battalion of the 502nd Parachute Infantry was ordered forward to hold the road to Bastogne at all costs. It was hoped that the defenders of Noville would be able to stream southward along that road to get into Bastogne.

2 platoon knew nothing of this as they moved steadily backward. Alan Bishop guided his men as best he could through the mists and the thick smoke of the gunfire, stumbling at times over uneven ground, but moving always with their faces and their carbines pointed at the enemy.

Max Gluber was in a savage mood. He had been firing carefully, watching as he dropped German after German. For himself, he would have stayed and died there, killing until he could kill no more. But he was a good soldier. He fell back with his comrades, telling himself that he could kill another day if he lived through this one.

To one side of him Joe Sullivan was shooting when he could see somebody to shoot at. This was like being in the ring, getting pounded by an opponent's fists. A man had to cover up at a time like that and wait until he could throw a punch himself.

"Dear God, just let me get through this," Lou Princezzi was whispering as he fired and ran, paused to fire again and then run on.

It seemed to him that this was all he had been doing for the past week. Shooting and running. At least he was still alive and uncaptured.

When he got back to Maria, if he ever did, he was going to spend a week in bed with her, just loving her up. Oh, they might pause to eat a little something and have a glass of wine ever so often just to give them strength to keep going. But all he wanted was her warm, soft flesh, to lose himself in it so he might forget this Hell through which he was running and remember that life consisted of something more than war.

Gawasowanee was enjoying himself. This shoot and run tactic was something he could understand and relish. Of course, he had Michelle to worry about, but she was always beside him, aping him.

If he stood and shot, she knelt beside him, watching. When he moved back, she was like his shadow, always a little in back of him. She breathed fitfully at times. She was deafened by the constant firing, but she was alive and she had begun to adore this big man with the red skin who took such good care of her.

They lay flat to the ground now with the girl snuggled up against his shoulder. He could feel her breath on his neck.

"You scared?" he asked softly, turning to look at her.

"A little," she whispered back.

He grinned. "I don't blame you. I'm scared myself."

"Not you," she said fiercely. "I watch you as you fight. You are having a good time. You like this fighting."

Gawasowanee smiled faintly. Maybe the girl was right. It was fun in a way, this shooting at krauts. Of course, it wasn't so much fun getting shot at, but what the hell! You had to take the bad with the good.

"You stay close to me, hear?" he said softly. "I don't want those krauts to capture you."

She nodded until her long yellow hair flew about. "You won't lose me. I'll be right beside you."

"All right. Now let's move back out of here."

They wriggled side by side over the ground and when Paul Andrews reckoned that it was safe to do so, they sprang to their feet and sprinted. The Belgian girl kept pace with him. She was a good runner, he thought.

When they had covered a hundred yards without a shot being fired at them, Gawasowanee moved his hand and they fell flat. He put his arm about her and held her close.

"You're a brave kid," he whispered.

"With you I am brave. If you weren't here, I would be so frightened, I would not be able to move."

He looked around him, wondering where the rest of the platoon might be. Then he saw a man running off to the right and recognized the sergeant.

Alan Bishop saw him at the same time, changed the direction of his run and came to flop down beside them.

"Where are the others?" he asked.

"Beats me. I lost them back a ways."

"We'll wait here. I want us to get together if we can."

They strained their eyes, trying to see. The main force of the battle was north of them now and moving westward. But there were enough Germans out there so that they knew they were still in a fight.

A running man caught their attention. That was Lou Princezzi. And there was Joe Sullivan close beside him. Alan hallooed, waving an arm, and they headed toward him.

Only Max Gluber was unaccounted for.

Max was bellydown in a hole, only his head poking out. He didn't want to get out of this fight, not while it still showed signs of continuing. He saw three white-clad Germans moving slowly and cautiously toward him, pausing to scan the seemingly empty land around them.

Max grinned coldly and slid his carbine forward slowly so as not to attract their attention by any sudden movement.

"Come on just a little closer, boys," he whispered. "Just another ten or twelve feet, that's all I ask."

They came on, their heads moving always, seeking out the Amerikaners. They had been ordered to kill, not to take any prisoners. But where were they? A man could not kill what he did not see.

They saw Max Gluber almost at the same time and their rifles came up. But Max was already firing by that time, a sharp burst that spat death at them from less than fifty yards. The Germans crumpled almost as one man and fell to the ground.

Max eyed them, then let his eyes run past them at the open ground. There were no more Germans. He nestled his gunstock against his cheek and fired another burst, watching the bodies jerk as that hot lead ploughed into them.

Then he rose to his feet and ran.

If Paulie were here, he might have scalped those men, but it was enough for him to know that they were dead. He ran bent over, pausing from time to time to let his eyes assess the land around him.

There was firing from behind him. He could hear the booming of the bigger guns, the sharp staccato bursts of fire from the Americans answering that gunfire. The damn fools, he thought, why don't they get out while they can?"

Maybe they couldn't. Maybe they were pinned down.

Max halted, turned back.

He saw a line of running men moving toward him. They were Americans, also fleeing from that major thrust of the Second Panzer Division. Paratroopers could do little against Mark IV tanks. One needed tank-destroyers or Sherman tanks for that. They were getting out to survive to fight another time.

Max waved an arm. they saw him, veered toward him.

"What's up?" a man called.

"All hell," Max grinned. "But we're all right on the fringe. Maybe we can get back to Bastogne."

When they came up to him, a lieutenant growled, "We just couldn't hold them. They had too much to throw at us."

Max nodded. "Let them go through. Let somebody else in this man's army do something to stop them."

The officer said, "This is one hell of a rest area. I came here to take it easy."

"So did we all. Come on, we can still make the road back into Bastogne—if the krauts haven't overrun it."

It was Lou Princezzi who saw them first. "Somebody coming," he called softly.

"Don't get nervous trigger fingers, boys. They're on our side."

He stood erect and waved, recognizing Max Gluber. Max waved back and yelled, "Found some pilgrims. We're joining up with you."

They rose up then and began to walk, merging with the men from the 10th Armored Division. They were tired men, all but exhausted. They had been fighting around the clock—forever, it seemed.

They headed south, hoping to hit the road. They moved along as briskly as tired muscles would allow, a few of them stumbling and muttering under their breaths as they recovered their balance. Somebody said, "I don't have more than five rounds left in my gun. God help us if we run into the krauts."

"I'll take care of you, Jimmy. I got eight rounds."

Tired smiles broke out upon the weatherbeaten faces.

Alan Bishop was walking between Joe Sullivan and Lou Princezzi. Joe was being gloomy, a rare thing for him.

"We'll never make it. We're all going to die," he kept muttering.

Lou growled at him, "No son-of-a-bitch of a kraut is going to kill me, Joe. I won't let him."

"How the hell can you stop him?"

"By killing the bastard first."

Joe Sullivan thought a moment, then nodded his head. "That makes sense," he agreed.

Alan Bishop chuckled. He was just as tired as the others and maybe that was why he saw humor in what Sullivan had just said. His eyes roamed arouind him, seeing the Mohawk with that girl hanging onto his arm, half running beside him, watching Max as he turned and looked back the way he had come with a savage fury darkening his face.

He called now, "Relax, Max. There'll be other days. You don't think the war is over, do you?"

"I don't like retreating."

Gawasowance called, "We aren't retreating, Maxie. We're just outflanking those bums. When we got 'em outflanked, we'll turn around and go back to kill them."

Michelle Kubeck pressed even closer to him. "Are you really going to continue fighting?"

"You bet we are. We're not licked, not by a long shot." At a sudden thought, he turned to her. "Hey, I didn't know you could talk American. Back there when I first met you, you stared at us as if you didn't know what we were saying."

"The good Father taught us at school. He said the English language was the most important one in the world because two great countries — England and the United States—spoke that language. And so I studied hard."

Paul Andrews smiled down at her. She was a pretty thing. In a few years she would probably be a real beauty—if she lived through the war. Anger flooded into him, anger against such a man as Adolf Hitler and these Germans who obeyed him so blindly.

He put his arm around the girl and gave her a squeeze.

"You keep on talking to me, honey. I like to hear your voice."

She looked at him and smiled. "You have a wife back in your country, yes?"

"Not me. Got a father and mother, two brothers—they're fighting against Japan right now—and a sister. No wife."

Her arm squeezed his. It occurred to Gawasowanee that maybe this blonde girl considered that he might be good husband material. He liked her—well, sure. Of course he did. But he did not want a wife. Besides she was a white girl and he was a Mohawk. It would never do. Still he could keep an eye on her, to make sure she lived through this goddam war.

"Tell me about yourself," he said.

As she chattered on about the farm and the cows they had owned, about the big spotted horse she had ridden from time to time, 2 platoon slogged on over the hard frozen ground. Now and then more men came up to join them, scattered remnants of units that had been stationed at Noville.

They came to the Bastogne road and moved along it.

Suddenly they heard a rumble of motors and saw advancing toward them what seemed to be an entire army.

They came to a stop, but only momentarily for someone shouted, "That's the 502nd parachute crowd."

Faced grimed with dirt and sweat broke into grins. They began to move forward again, waving their arms at the Parachute Infantry. They had joined up with units of their own army. They were no longer wandering around in a world where the krauts might appear out of nowhere.

Gawasowanee hugged Michelle. "We're safe now, honey. For a time, anyhow."

The girl laughed.

They moved onward, southbound on the road. From moment to moment someone from the 502nd would shout out at them.

"We'll take care of you guys. Just keep walking."

"When they needed some real men up here, they sent for the five-oh-two bunch."

Max Gluber snarled, but Joe Sullivan chuckled, calling back, "You're welcome to it, buddy. We left a little for you guys to mop up."

"We're not hogs," Lou Princezzi added.

Now they could see Bastogne, the wrecked buildings, the scattering of armor that had come here to fight a last ditch stand. A car with somebody important in it—a general, to judge by the stars on his helmet—came speeding toward them. When the car was within a few feet of them, the driver braked.

"Where are you men from? Noville?"

Sergeant Alan Bishop saluted. "Yes, sir. We pulled out to prevent getting captured."

The sharp eyes studied him, the others. A faint smile touched the general's lips. "So you can fight another day, eh?"

"Yes, sir. We won't do our side any good in a prisoner of war camp."

The general made a wry face. "Have you heard what happened at Malmedy? The Germans gunned down a hundred and twenty-five of our soldiers who had surrendered."

"No, sir. I hadn't heard."

"Pass the word. It doesn't pay to surrender to those

animals."

"I will, sir."

He saluted again, the driver gunned the motor and the car moved off. Max Gluber came up to his side and stood looking after the command car with a thoughtful expression.

"Did I hear right, Sarge? Did those krauts murder a hundred and twenty-five of our men? In cold blood?"

"You heard right, Max."

The German Jew glanced at him, his face set and grim, his eyes hard. "Can you blame me for not wanting to take prisoners? They aren't men. They're not members of the human race, those krauts. Hitler's got them mesmerized."

"You know, Maxie, I don't think I'll take any more prisoners either. Let the pigs die on the battlefield, they want to fight so much."

It was a sullen platoon that made its way toward Bastogne. But for the grace of God and a lucky Providence, they themselves might well have been numbered among those martyred hundred and twenty-five men. They slogged along and they thought, and those thoughts were of killing men who murdered defenseless people in that way.

5

Bastogne was chaos. Everywhere one looked, there were soldiers resting, seated on the ground or lying flat, the lines of weariness etched sharply in their gaunt faces. They lay beside their rifles or their carbines and while they might sleep, their bodies twitched and moved as though even in their dreams they were out there in the cold, fighting off the Germans.

Michelle was tugging on Paul Andrews' arm as they went into the town. Her eyes were running here and there among the houses and down the streets.

"This way," she whispered, "come on, this way."

"Where to, little one?" asked the Mohawk.

"I know a place where we can go."

He stared down at her. "What place?"

"My uncle's house—if it's still standing. He will be glad to see me, happy to welcome you Americans."

"You got an uncle here?"

"My father's brother. I haven't seen him for quite a long time though. I don't even know if he's alive or dead, but I have to find out."

Gawasowanee waved an arm at the others. "Over here, we're going with Michelle."

Alan Bishop looked at him. "She know this place?"

"Got an uncle living here, or so she says."

They trailed after him, walking leaden-footed, their eyes dulled by tiredness, their bodies just slouching along. They paid no heed to the clatter of tanks and half-tracks, or to the other soldiers they passed who were just wandering around waiting for orders.

There seemed to be no sense of direction in anyone. Eyes stared at them blearily, without interest, as if they had lost interest in what went on around them. These men needed rest and food. They were on the verge of exhaustion.

Alan Bishop shook his head. Nobody here was in condition to fight off the Germans when they came to take Bastogne. These men were nothing but automatons going through the motions of living. He himself felt tiredness rising in his body, all he wanted was to flop down and sleep.

Sleep! It seemed years since he had enjoyed a full night's sleep, years since he had taken an interest in anything but killing Germans and staying alive. After a time all that became a sort of habit.

Joe Sullivan plodded along head down. He didn't care where they were going or what they were going to do. All he asked of life now was somewhere to lie down. Jees! What was it like to drop and close your eyes and just let the weariness inside you wash across your brain and muscles? Did men really sleep anymore? Or did they just walk as he walked, half stumbling at every stride?

Lou Princezzi wanted to dream. He wanted to hold Maria in his arms in those dreams, to kiss and love her as he had done back there at Niagara Falls. Did people sleep anymore? Sure they did, somewhere in the world. He wondered what it would be like, just to lie down and let the world slide away from him.

Max Gluber was exhausted, too, but he still held that hate inside him, and his hate for the Germans sustained him. There would come a time to rest, as soon as he had killed all the Germans in the world. He thought about killing Germans all the way to the big house on a side street.

He paused and stared up at the house in something like surprise, moving from side to side in his tiredness. He watched Michelle run forward, dragging the Mohawk with her.

She pounded on the door, using both fists, crying out, "Uncle Derek! Uncle Derek! Are you there? Aunt Matilda!"

Paul Andrews leaned his shoulder against the wall, looking down at her. Her face was tense, partly frightened. He wondered what it might be like for a homeless girl to come to the house where her uncle lived—and find him dead. The house was as quiet as a tomb.

"Maybe they're out," he said quietly.

She shook her head. "They would not go out together. At least—I don't believe they would."

Then a voice called from behind the door, "Who is it?"

Michelle began to cry. The tears rolled down her cheeks as she choked out, "It is I! Michelle! Please, Aunt Matilda, open the door."

There was a soft cry, the metallic sound of a bar being drawn back, and then a woman in her thirties was standing there, eyes wide and mouth slightly open, her eyes brimming with tears.

"Michelle! My little Michelle!"

Her arms embraced the girl, strained her to her bosom. She kissed her cheeks, her forehead, whispering, "You are alive. Alive! I did not think ever to see you again. We heard that the Germans had overrun your farm."

"The Germans came. I ran, as did the others. I found the American soldiers. Mamma, Papa—I do not know about them. I—I am afraid they are dead."

Matilda Kubek stared past the girl at the dirty, bearded soldiers in their torn, stained combat uniforms. Her eyes widened.

"You are Americans! Was it you who found my Michelle? Come in, come in!"

Michelle reached out for Paul Andrews. "This is the man who found me, who protected me," she murmured.

Gawasowanee grinned, showing strong white teeth. "She brought us luck. She's some girl."

Matilda Kubek frowned, glancing from face to face, and Michelle broke in, laughing. "He is a very brave man, my Paul. He has killed so many Germans, I could not count them. All the time I was beside him, hugging myself against him. They are all brave, these Americans."

Matilda Kubek glanced again at the faces behind her niece. "You are tired, very tired from the fighting. Come in, please. You shall all have beds in which to sleep."

The Mohawk grinned when Michelle translated.

"Ma'am, you couldn't have made us happier." He turned to the others. "She has beds for us. Let's go."

It was Michelle who guided them upstairs and into several large bedrooms. She stood and watched as they dropped their gear and just lay down on top of the beds. Only Paul Andrews did not join them. She tugged him out into the hall and closed the other door behind her.

Her blue eyes glinted with laughter. "I am going to put you in my own bed," she whispered.

Paul Andrews blinked. If she had been a little older, he might have gotten a charge out of that, but she was so young. She couldn't be more than fourteen. He smiled down at her.

"If it is your bed," he said, "I shall be honored. I'm

sure it's a soft one."

She caught his hand in hers and drew him down the hall toward an end room. Opening the door, she all but dragged him into it. It was a very pleasant room with a blue carpet on the floor and window curtains in blue and white. There was a matching spread on the big double bed.

"Get undressed and get between the sheets," she ordered. "You will be able to sleep just as long as you want."

She went to the bed and began to turn down the blankets and the spread, disclosing the white sheets. Almost against his will the Mohawk found himself studying her body.

She was nicely curved. She had great legs and nice hips and while her breasts were small, they showed promise of maturing into something more than mere bumps. Her dress was stained and ragged. He could catch a glimpse of bare flesh there at her side.

Better not think about her that way though. She was much too young.

"There," she nodded, standing back.

The Mohawk waited. Wasn't she going to leave the room? After all, if she wanted him to strip down and get into those sheets, she was going to have to get out in the hall.

An impish look came into her eyes and she giggled. "I am sorry. I forgot that men are so modest. I will go away now and leave you alone."

She came across the room to him, stood on her tiptoes and pressed her young mouth to his lips. Then she was out in the hall, closing the door behind her.

Gawasowanee scowled. He wished she hadn't done that, kissing him that way. It stirred emotions in him he had all but forgotten. He shrugged and began to undress.

While 2 platoon slept, the war went on.

In the south, General George S. Patton was wheeling his third Army to the north. Wherever he could, he borrowed men and sent them up toward Bastogne, including the 4th and 5th Infantry Divisions along with the 10th Armored. Behind them he had the 35th Infantry and the 6th Armored Division.

To the north above the Bulge was Field Marshal Sir Bernard Montgomery with his English troops, and American forces under Major General Matthew Ridgeway. Montgomery did not believe in the seriousness of the German attack: he felt that there would be another attack, probably against his own troops.

Yet he swung his troops around to the south, to deal with the advancing German armored columns, followed so closely by their troops. From the west troops were hurriedly scraped together and thrown into action against the foremost of the German units which had penetrated beyond Rochefort almost to the Meuse River.

There was no dismay at Allied Headquarters. By this time, it was realized that what had first been thought to be a diversionary tactic was, in effect, an all-out offensive. There were German tanks and German armies everywhere in Belgium, from Monschau and Trois Ponts to Diekirch and Ettelbruck in the south.

Bastogne alone was holding out.

Yet Bastogne was surrounded by Germans. It was an island in a sea of attack. To defend it, Brigadier General Anthony McAuliffe had only exhausted men on whom to count.

Yet Allied Command saw its chance to attack the enemy in its extended position. Catch them, crack them between the armies under Montgomery and the armies under Patton: this was the plan.

Bastogne, of course, commanded the roads over which the enemy must move in order to fulfill the timetable set for it. The German high command had never anticipated that they would be held up in such a manner. They had tanks and troops waiting to move. Bastogne was holding up the movements of those tanks and troops. Bastogne must be removed.

To defend Bastogne, McAuliffe had four regiments, four light artillery battalions and two howitzer battalions. Together with this array he had at his disposal the 420th Armored Field Artillery Battalion with some of the 10th Armored Division. He also had about forty big tanks and a few light tanks. There was also the 705th Tank Destroyer Battalion.

Grouped against him was the German 26th Volksgrenadiers with the Panzer Lehr Division, the 901st Panzer Grenadiers and the 77th and 78th regiments.

On the morning of December 22, four German officers under a white truce flag drove up the Arlon road from Remonfosse. They were stopped by Company F whose duty at the moment it was to guard that road.

Two of the officers were taken to Major Jones, commander of the 327th Glider Infantry. They handed him a note.

Jones took the note to Division Headquarters in Bastogne. He handed the note to General McAuliffe who read it and in digust, growled, "Nuts!"

The note demanded the surrender of Bastogne.

General McAuliffe looked at his officers. They looked back at him. He had no intention of surrendering. He was here to stop the German thrust as best he could, but how could he reply to their demand?

"Any ideas?" he asked the men around him.

Lieutenant Colonel Kinnard began to grin. "That first remark of yours ought to do, sir."

"Oh? What was that?"

"You said 'Nuts!' "

General McAuliffe began to laugh. "Why not? We'll send it."

Colonel Joseph Harper, who commanded the 327th Glider Infantry Regiment, was sent for. He was shown the German demand for surrender. When he had read it and then looked inquiringly at his commanding officer, McAuliffe produced his reply.

Colonel Harper was delighted and volunteered to deliver the reply himself. He went back to where the German officers were waiting and gave them the note.

They read it, their faces puzzled.

"Nuts?" one of them asked doubtfully.

"In other words," Harper smiled tigerishly, "go to hell."

"You are a fool. We will annihilate you," growled one of the officers.

"On your way," Harper gestured.

The word went up and down the lines. The general had replied, "Nuts!" to the German demand for their surrender. Everywhere there was laughter. Leave it to the general to think up an answer like that! He was talking for them all, for every man in his command, officer and private alike.

Nuts to the Germans. Nuts to their demands.

If they wanted to take Bastogne, they were going to have to fight for it. They would kill Americans, but by God!—the Americans would kill a hell of a lot of Krauts, too.

Something like new energy came to the men in Bastogne. They were here to face the whole might of the German Army. Let them come. They would give them a welcome the whole world would never forget.

Nuts to Adolph Hitler!

Paul Andrews was dreaming of his homeland—not the streets of New York City and the high-rise buildings on which he had worked, but the soft, quiet woods up around Great Sacandaga Lake—and of the animals he had hunted there in his youth.

There was a bear he had trailed and as he moved toward him his rifle poised for shooting, the bear lunged at him. He wrapped his arms about the bear, trying to keep it from tearing out his backbone with its long claws. . . .

"Oh, please," the bear whispered.

Gawasowanee opened his eyes. He was holding Michelle in his arms, all but crushing her body to his own. For an instant, still lost in his dream, he stared down at her blankly.

She began to giggle. Paul Andrews noted also that she was not struggling to get away. He also noted that his body was responding to the closeness of her own. He could feel the smoothness of her thighs, the bump of her belly, the hard nipples of her tiny breasts.

"I'm sorry," he gasped, trying to move away.

She pouted at him, her blue eyes wet with laughter. "What is to be sorry about? You were having a dream, yes? And in the dream you reached out and grabbed me."

"You were a bear," he muttered.

Her dancing eyes widened. "A bear? One of those big, shaggy things that live in the woods?"

He nodded glumly. He wanted to put his arms around her and drag her in against him, to hold her close. Oh, not in any carnal way—at least, he did not believe so—

but because she was another human being and he was tired of war and he liked lying here in this warm bed with this girl.

"I am prettier than a bear, I should hope," she went on, her lips curved with a smile.

"Of course you are. You're beautiful."

"You really think so?"

Gawasowanee grinned. "You know I do, you little witch. You're the most beautiful girl I've ever seen."

She nodded. "I am glad you think so."

"But you're only a child."

Her eyes stared at him. "I am not a child, my big Indian. Oh, I know you think I am. But I am not."

She came a little closer in the bed and no matter how he tried, he could not get away from her warm young body. It almost rested against his own and his body went on reacting to it.

"I'd better be getting up," he said.

She flung her arms about him and nestled even closer. "No. Just stay here, like this. Isn't this nice?"

"Too nice," he mumbled.

She lifted her head and peered down into his eyes. "Why are you afraid of me?"

"You're just a child. A man doesn't—well, he doesn't do things with a child that he might with a woman."

Michelle scowled. "I am a woman. I am! I am!"

"In another year or two—maybe."

Her full mouth pouted at him. Paul Andrews wished she would not do that, because it went on stirring the fires in his flesh and he knew that he must not do anything with this girl. Not that he did not want to! There was something about her, some elemental appeal, that stirred his very bones.

"You saved my life, you know," she went on

dreamily. "That means I belong to you. I am yours."

"Now look—"

Her soft palm covered his mouth. Almost against his will, he found himself kissing it. Her blue eyes laughed down at him.

"Yes, do that. Kiss me."

"Michelle, listen. You are underage. If you were older. . . ."

"So? What would you do if I were older?"

A man can stand just so much temptation. This girl was plastering her soft body against his, egging him on, and if she didn't get away from him damn soon, he was not going to be responsible for what might happen.

Almost of its own will, his arm tightened about her, bringing her down closer against him, so that she lay almost on top of his body. He felt the pressure of her thigh against that male part of him and he knew from her sudden gasp that she understood how much he wanted her.

They stared into each other's eyes for a long moment. Then Michelle let her head dip downward until her mouth was against his own. They kissed.

Gawosowanee thought the top of his head would blow off. Never before had he wanted a female the way he wanted this pretty blonde girl. But he must not have her. She was a child. In a few more years she would be a grown woman. But right now she was a kid.

His hands caught her shoulders and pushed her away. He held her like that, above him, and he saw the dazed look in her face.

"I knew it," she whispered softly. "I knew it would be like that—with you."

"Get out of bed," he breathed. "Goddamn it, Michelle! I'm only human. You know what they'd do to me if you and I were to do what we both want to do?

They'd hang me. Or shoot me. I'm not sure which."

Her eyes stared down into his, filled with love and understanding. She might be a child in years, Paul Andrews thought, but she was a woman, deep inside her. She understood the way he felt, she knew the way she was feeling, right now. She stirred slightly, almost as though she meant to press herself against him again.

Instead she drew away, crouching on the bed with the covers above her. Now he could see she was wearing a skimpy cotton nightgown that clung to her body. It was short. It only went down to the middle of her thighs and he saw that her nipples were taut against it.

"I will go now," she breathed, and moved to get out of bed.

As she did so, her nightgown lifted slightly so that he caught a glimpse of her thigh, and her hip. Then she was on the floor, looking down at him.

Paul Andrews closed his eyes. Maybe she didn't know how thin that nightgown really was. He heard her laugh softly.

"You are afraid of me, aren't you?" she whispered. "You want me, don't you? I can tell. I may be only a child, but I am also on the verge of being a woman. Good! I want you to want me, my big Indian."

There was a little silence.

Carefully Gawasowanee opened his eyes. She was standing there clinging to the frilled hem of the nightgown as if about to lift it over her head. Her eyes were very big, very bright.

"Do you want to see me?" she whispered.

"No!"

The word burst from his mouth, yet in that same moment, he knew he lied. He wanted very much to see her, to grab her and drag her down onto the bed and play with her. He did not dare.

He said softly, "Wait. I do want to see you, Michelle. God knows I do. But I don't dare."

She smiled down at him. "You do not trust yourself, you mean. I like that. Very well, then, I will not tease you any more."

Michelle turned away, walked toward a bathroom door. Her hips wagged back at him. Then, just as she opened the door and with her back turned toward him, she yanked off the nightgown.

Paul Andrews tried to avert his eyes, but the sight of that pale white body held him hypnotized. Not until her hand closed the door did he blink.

God help me, he thought. If we stay here in this house another night, I won't be responsible for what might happen.

6

Sergeant Alan Bishop rose quietly from the bed where he had been sleeping. He felt refreshed, though there was still an ache deep inside him. His glance took in the three men slumbering in the room.

Let them sleep. He wanted to get out of the house to see for himself what the situation was. He picked up his carbine and moved from the room, closing the door quietly behind him.

There were sounds from belowstairs, together with the appetizing smell of bacon cooking. That told him how hungry he was. He went down the steps easily, turned at an open doorway, and saw the dining room.

Matilda Kubek was standing beside the table, putting plates on it, with knives and forks. Her face lighted up at the sight of him.

She began to speak, but realized that he might not understand her, so she gestured at a chair and made motions to indicate that he should seat himself. Then she hurried into the kitchen.

Within moments she was back again, carrying a plate heaped with eggs and bacon and potatoes. She said something in her native language and Alan Bishop wondered if she spoke French.

"Merci," he said. *"Oeufs au lard. C'est tres bien."*

Her face beamed. "Ah, you speak French! I am so glad. It is very difficult to deal with people when you and they cannot talk with one another."

Alan grinned. "I'm not as good at it as I wish. I learned it at school and then I took a cram course in it while we were waiting in England."

She sat down and folded her hands. "How is the battle going, Sergeant? Do you think the Germans will overrun Bastogne?"

Alan swallowed a mouthful of the food. It was delicious. He said, "Not if we can stop them—and I think we can. We're sure going to try."

Her smile was radiant. "God bless you Americans. I remember the last world war. I was only a small girl, of course, but I remember papa in uniform, and the Boches—that was what we called the Germans in those days—and the fighting that went on. It was terrible, though I think not as terrible as the fighting that is now taking place."

"These are bad times for you, but they'll be over some day. You just have to hang on until that day comes."

She nodded, glancing around her. "I pray God every night that he will spare my home. I see no reason why I should be spared when so many others have lost theirs—Michelle is one of those—but who knows the divine will?"

There were footsteps on the stairs and Max Gluber came into the room with Lou Princezzi. Their faces lighted up at the sight of the food and Madame Kubek rose to hurry out into the kitchen.

"Smells good," Max said as he seated himself.

Alan grinned, "We owe a lot to the Indian. Hadn't been for him and that girl, we wouldn't be here."

Lou nodded. "When this war gets finished, I want all the platoon guys to come to my house for a spaghetti dinner. Maria and I will do it up brown."

Max growled, "When this is finished," he sighed,

"there will be fighting for a long time to come, I think."

"Half a year, no more," Alan muttered. "Way I figure it, this business in the Ardennes is Hitler's last gasp."

"If he doesn't win by it," Lou murmured.

Alan glanced at him. "You're just tired, Lou. Hitler is finished. He just doesn't know it yet."

"Didn't feel like that to me, not out there," Max Gluber said. "He threw a lot of armor and troops at us."

"And we spoiled their looks. Sure, sure, they're knocking us around—but Hell! We were here to rest, not to fight. Wait until Patton ties into those tanks and troops. And Ridgeway from up north."

"I sure hope you're right," Lou grinned.

Madame Kubek came in with two plates heaped high with bacon, eggs and potatoes. She put them before Lou and Max with a faint smile.

"Eat well," she murmured in her native tongue.

"Where's Sullivan?" Alan asked.

"Still pounding the pillow."

"And Paulie?"

"Don't know. He didn't sleep with us."

"I got to go out and find out what the brass wants us to do. Soon as they show up, tell them to get ready to move out."

Lou looked at him. "Move out? To where? The krauts are all around us."

Alan Bishop picked up his carbine. "Then we got to get moving and kill some more of them."

He paused to glance into the kitchen where Matilda Kubek was making more coffee. She turned and smiled at him, saying, "You will have another cup before you leave?"

"You make it sound very tempting."

Her shrug stirred her breasts. It made Alan Bishop realize that it had been a long time since he had talked with a woman. Hell! If they needed him and 2 platoon, he would get the word soon enough.

"A second cup would go great," he smiled. "I would like it if you had a cup with me."

She nodded. "Thank you. I would like that."

They were enjoying their coffee when Michelle and Paul Andrews came downstairs. Alan looked sharply at their faces, seeing what he thought was happiness in them. Something stirred inside him, a protest that he smothered.

Had they slept together last night? If they had. . . oh, what the Hell. What difference did it make? They were young and healthy, both of them. The only trouble was, the girl was a little too young.

The sergeant decided he would mind his own business while he watched as Michelle practically pushed the Indian into a chair and then ran out into the kitchen.

Paul Andrews asked, "Well, what do we do now?"

"I'm going out to search around and try to get orders," Alan nodded. "There ought to be something for us to do."

Lou chuckled. "Sure. Rest up."

Max Gluber growled, "You can do a lot of that when the war is over."

"I can, but I'd appreciate it more right now. Man, I'm still bushed."

"Go back to bed then," Alan told him, lifting his carbine and moving toward the front door.

The cold struck him when he went out into the street. He had forgotten that it was December, only a few days until Christmas. How nice it would be if he could only go back inside and stay for a few days.

He liked Madame Kubek and wondered where her

husband might be. What was it Michelle had called him? Uncle Derek. There had been no sign of him. Maybe the man was dead.

He moved toward headquarters, seeing it located in a mostly one-story high building with small windows. It looked to Alan Bishop like a small factory. To the west there was a flat plain about a mile long and beyond it were rows of evergreen trees. Anything that moved toward them from that direction would make good targets.

He turned and began his walk, seeing the town itself, and the spire of the church rising upward from among the rooftops. There was a graveyard off to one side. Convenient, Alan thought as he moved along. At least they could bury their dead.

When he was almost at the doorway of the headquarters building, a major came out and began striding toward him. Alan saluted.

"A platoon reporting for duty, sir."

The major ran his eyes over him. "Are you all there is of it?"

"No, sir. Some of us are billeted in a private house, others are scattered here and there."

"Can you round them up?"

"Yes, sir."

"Do that. Get them ready for a fight. The Germans are out there hidden by those trees." He pointed across the flat land toward the evergreens. "Get them to cover, whatever cover you can find. And—stop the sons-of-bitches."

Alan grinned and saluted. The major moved off and Alan trotted back to the Kubek house. By this time, Paul Andrews was finished with his breakfast and was talking to Michelle who was staring at him with big eyes and sipping at her coffee.

"Time to move out," Alan said. "We got us some fighting to do."

Max Gluber was on his feet, his face losing its glumness. "Are they coming, Sarge?"

"So headquarters seems to think."

Lou Princezzi sighed and reached for his carbine. There was no rest for the weary. It was always like this lately. No sooner did they get a chance to relax than whammo!—they were in the thick of the battle again.

Joe Sullivan only grunted as he followed Max onto the street. He breathed deep of the cold air. At least, it wasn't summer with the sweat running all over you and the damned heat sapping your energies.

Michelle's hands clasped those of the Indian. "You must go? So soon?"

"There's a war on, honey. But I'll be back, the Great Manitou willing."

She crossed herself. "I shall say prayers all day long."

Alan said, "You do that, Michelle. We need all we can get."

Then they were moving down the street toward the stone wall that enclosed the cemetery. Alan ran his eyes over that wall. It was thick. It would stop anything short of a direct hit from an .88. That was where he wanted to be.

All around them other men were moving forward to form the perimeter of a defense for Bastogne. The men of the 101st Parachute team were side by side with those of the 501st Regiment and some elements of the 9th and 10th Armored Divisions. There was no talk among the men, only grim faces peered out from under their helmets. Every man knew what was coming at them. They were going to have to fight like hell just to stay alive.

Alan led his platoon into the graveyard, walking down the narrow pathways between the tombstones. He brought them to the stone fence and there they all crouched down, resting their carbines on the capstones of the wall.

Joe Sullivan looked around him and saw the wall lined with men. Not just the 101st was here, but men from other divisions, too. All ready, all waiting for the attack they knew was on its way—or soon would be.

There was a rumble from the town square and they heard the tank-destroyers moving into position with here and there a Sherman tank among them. That was good. They would have the weight of all that heavy stuff behind them, throwing their shells at the enemy.

Max Gluber didn't look around as some of the others did. His eyes were focused on those distant evergreens. The krauts would come out of those trees when they came. He wanted to be ready to gun down as many of them as he could.

Lou Princezzi was not thinking of anything. Last night he had lain in bed and thought about Maria until his very guts ached. If only he could be with her for just a little time! Ha! If he were to see her and hold her in his arms, he would never be able to come back here and fight.

Christ! Why did men have to fight and kill each other? What was there about humanity that made them worse than animals? Even animals were not fighting all the time. Just at the mating season, sometimes, and then it was only a battle to see who got the females.

Animals rarely killed each other except for food. He smiled wryly wondering how a dead German would taste. Men didn't even have the excuse of hunger for all this shooting and killing. It was just because one man— that goddamned Adolf Hitler!—wanted Germany to rule the world that he was here.

He nestled his cheek against his gun. He would kill all the Germans he could this day. The sooner they all did that, the sooner the war would be over and he would be back with Maria.

Paul Andrews was remembering how Michelle had looked that morning, naked. Her body belied the fact that she was only fourteen. Of course, he had only seen her from the rear, but that was pretty damn good. Why the hell couldn't she be at least sixteen?

He grinned. Maybe it was just as well she was only fourteen. If she really were sixteen, when they had been so close together in that bed, he might not have acted as gentlemanly as he had.

Something moved out there in the woods.

"Here they come," he whispered.

Max Gluber tensed. Trust the eyes of the Indian to see something he could not. He slid his carbine forward and waited.

There was a distant rumble. The tanks were coming. Behind them there would be the kraut soldiers. Their job was to get the soldiers and let the tank-destroyers and the Shermans attend to the heavy stuff.

The huge Mark IV tanks came first, rumbling between the trees, advancing steadily. Their cannon began to talk and the men behind the stone walls heard the booming of those guns and then the whistle of the shells overhead. Behind them the tank-destroyers and the Shermans began to open up.

A big Mark IV tank exploded, showering metal in all directions. Two others slowed to pump more shells into the town.

Now the white-clad forms of the Germans in their winter war gear moved forward. Either they did not see the men behind the stone walls or they thought they could sweep them away. They advanced at a half-trot, meeting no resistance.

They were a hundred yards away now.

"Let the bastards have it," somebody snapped.

Instantly the carbines and the rifles opened fire. They sent a hail of lead across that mile of flat land sweeping away the Germans who dropped, some of them, with one leg off the ground as they walked. They went down and they lay there in stiff, contorted attitudes.

Max Gluber was like an automaton. He fired a burst, peered through the smoke, fired another burst. He was an efficient killing machine with no pity, no thought for the men he cut down. They were here to kill him, but he was the one who would do all the killing.

On all sides of him men fired as he did, mowing down the lines of enemy infantry advancing against them. Here and there a man was sobbing in the intensity of his concentration. Those men out there must not be allowed into Bastogne. They were the Germans, the men who wanted to rule the world.

The Hell with them! They weren't going to rule anybody, not if the Americans behind the stone walls or dug into the foxholes could prevent it. The rattle and roar of the guns went on. Their sound filled the world.

There was no other world but this, no place that existed save for this land around a tiny Belgium city where the krauts were throwing their everything at the Americans in their desperate attempt to seize it.

Joe Sullivan was grinning. He did not realize this, but it was the same grin that used to infuriate his opponents in the ring. He was swinging haymakers with every round he fired and he could see his man go down every time.

"Got you," he would whisper every so often. "Come on, the bell's rung and the fight's on. Come and get it, you goddamn bastards."

He was hardened to killing by this time. At first over there in England where they had waited for D-Day, he had been worried about himself. It was all right to hit a man with boxing gloves—oh, there had been accidents, but never to him.

He had not been sure he could really kill a man with the carbine he had been issued. Well, that had been a long time ago. Now it was different. You killed men out there just to stay alive. They died and you lived. Hopefully. The more of them you killed, the better were your chances of staying alive.

Joe Sullivan had not understood Max Gluber and his hatred of the Germans at first. Oh, sure, he knew Max was a Jew, knew also that Hitler had killed six million Jews in his concentration camps. But that had never affected Joe very much.

But now! Now that he had seen the krauts in action, now that he had heard of the massacred soldiers they had cut down defenseless men with their arms up, he had developed a hatred of his own. It was good to see them drop before your fire, good to see them lying there in the attitudes of death.

Kill all you could. A dozen, two dozen. As many as fifty. What difference did it make? They sent more men at you, to die. Joe never blamed the men he killed. It was the others, the ones higher up who sent them on to die that he blamed.

He wished he could get Hitler in his sights. By God! That would be something.

Paul Andrews did not care much for this sort of fighting. He liked it when he was out on a patrol, where stealth and an ability to remain unseen counted most. But he could shoot. He had been able to shoot since he was a little tyke back on the reservation.

The only difference between then and now was that he did not kill to eat. He killed now to prevent his getting killed. He lay there and aimed, using his carbine as an extension of himself, hurling out death at those who came to kill him.

There were smoking tanks here and there on the field, some of them still burned. The Germans were using those tanks as tiny forts from behind which to shoot and hide. No matter. Once the fighting stopped and the order came to withdraw, they would show themselves.

Behind the firing troops, the tank-destroyers and the Shermans were hurling their shells. They would scream overhead and then there was a *thunnk* as they hit, and after that the explosion. Noise was everywhere. It all but shattered the eardrums.

Alan Bishop glanced around him. His men were all here. He could make out only one or two who had been hit, lying on the ground behind the wall. The trouble with a battle was you knew what was going on around you, but what about the rest of the fight? Was it going as well for them as it was for the men here who crouched behind this stone wall?

Somebody yelled hoarsely, then shouted, "Here they come!"

Alan Bishop risked a look, raising his head above the capstone. His mouth fell open. It seemed that the whole goddamn kraut army was running toward them.

He opened his mouth to yell a warning, but it was not needed. His men had seen the enemy. Instantly the automatic rifles and the carbines opened up. Like a hail, that leaden burst cut down the men moving toward them. It was as if a scythe had swept their feet out from under them.

Yet more came on, running past the dead bodies littering the ground. Here and there a man stumbled over one. They fired as they advanced, but their bullets either went high or ricocheted off the stone wall. It was a stupid thing to do, sending those soldiers in against them in such a charge, Alan told himself, but he was not a man to argue with the German High Command.

Apparently the enemy felt that a determined assault could carry the day. It was up to the Americans here to convince the German High Command differently.

Somebody growled, "I'm running low on ammo."

"Me, too," another voice answered.

God Almighty! Surely it wasn't going to be because of a shortage of ammunition that the Germans were going to be able to take Bastogne! A man could fight until he died, but only if he had something to fight with. An empty carbine or automatic weapon wasn't of much use except as a club.

The firing went on though. Here and there a man picked up a fallen gun, used that.

Now the field before them was littered with dead Germans. They lay in windrows, sometimes in little heaps, mute testimony to the firepower of the American forces opposing them.

A silence hovered over the battlefield now. No more Germans came against them. Only the dead bodies and the shattered hulks of the Mark IV tanks littered that open space.

Men lay back on the ground behind the stone wall, some of them with their eyes closed, breathing deeply, letting the excitement and the killing fever ease out of them. They had held Bastogne for one more day. Could they hold it for another?

Not without ammo, they couldn't.

And all around Bastogne there were only enemy soldiers and enemy armor. All roads in or out were closed to them. They were completely surrounded.

Joe Sullivan glanced sideways at Max Gluber and he grinned. "Had enough of killing Germans for today, Maxie?"

"I can never have enough of that. But I need more bullets. I'm running too damned low."

"Me, too. I guess we all are. And this damn fog keeps getting colder all the time."

Paul Andrews looked around him, aware for the first time of that cold Arctic air sweeping in. The fog that had lifted for a time was getting thicker. It was growing harder to see anybody who was more than ten feet away.

"Great time for the krauts to advance," he muttered. "This fog would hide them until they were on top of us."

"Their tough luck," granted Lou Princezzi.

Lou shivered in his combat jacket. He wished he had something warmer to put on. He didn't mind fighting, but he liked to be comfortable while he was doing it. He also wished that he could build a fire. But that was forbidden: the light would give the krauts something to shoot at.

Still, if they couldn't see the enemy, the enemy sure as hell couldn't see them. Maybe they had a few hours of respite.

They waited for orders, shivering, their hands gripping their guns.

7

Captain Jim Buxton was in a quandary. He stood outside headquarters studying the fog that rolled in across Bastogne. Would the Germans take advantage of that fog to come in with all guns blazing? Or would they use its cover to regroup, to bring up reinforcements, and then attack when they had clear weather by which to see?

It was up to him. "Use your judgment, Jim," his superior had told him. "If you think you can get away with it, take out a patrol and find out what they mean to do."

Captain Buxton signed. If he went out with some men and didn't come back, he was offering up their lives needlessly. On the other hand, if he were to contact the Germans, perhaps discover something about their plans, then it would all be worthwhile.

"I ought to flip a coin," he told himself morosely.

They hadn't taught him anything like that at West Point. His instructors had assured him that a logical thinking out of any plan, weighing all the pros and cons, would lead to the proper decision.

The hell with that! He reached into a pocket and brought out a quarter. He flipped it. It landed on his palm, heads up. He made a face. He was going out.

He moved forward along the road with the graveyard to his right. His eyes were caught by the figure of Sergeant Alan Bishop where he lounged with his back to the stone wall. He recalled Alan Bishop from their fighting days near Antwerp and knew him to be a good, sound man.

He crossed the graveyard, crouching low so as not to attract the attention of an enemy sniper.

"Sergeant, I want a patrol—just a few men—to come with me out there." He nodded at the mile-distant forest.

"Yes, sir. Lou, Paul, Max, Joe."

The men came out of their relaxed attitude, their eyes focused on Captain Buxton accusingly. The captain squirmed mentally. What right had he to subject these men who had faced death a thousand or more times in the past year to go out there where the full might—or almost the full might—of the Fifth Panzer Army would be arrayed against them?

It was like asking men to lie down and die.

Yet they obeyed orders. They came to their feet with their carbines in their hands and they followed Captain Buxton as he crept to the opening in the cemetery wall and then out of it toward the field that lay shrouded in mists.

Nobody said a word. If some crackbrain back there at headquarters had thought up this patrol, that was his business. Their job was to go through with it. But to these men of 2 platoon, it seemed damned stupid.

Lou Princezzi was thinking that everybody in Bastogne knew where the krauts were. Out there behind those evergreen trees. They had tanks and a hell of a lot of men. What the hell else was there to discover?

Max Gluber did not mind. Indeed, he was secretly pleased at going on such a mission. It would give him a chance, he hoped, to gun down a few more Germans. His hands tightened on his carbine until his knuckles showed white.

Joe Sullivan followed Alan as he had followed him

ever since their first drop into enemy-held territory. It was not for him to think, it was up to him to follow where Sarge led and to fight when they found the enemy.

Only Gawasowanee was happy. He enjoyed this part of the war. He liked to go out on patrols, where his own special skills, inherited from his Mohawk ancestors, gave him something of an advantage.

His eyes scanned the fog and he paused from time to time to listen. Sometimes he even lifted his head and sniffed.

Alan watched him, knowing that he was his best man on such a job. What all his other men, himself included, would not notice, would be clear as glass to the Mohawk. So when Gawasowanee lifted his left hand suddenly, Alan froze, and gestured the others to silence.

Captain Buxton began to feel that the sergeant was the man in command here. He was a veteran. He had made any number of these scouting trips before and he seemed to defer to the man with the dark red skin.

As he crouched beside Bishop, the captain whispered, "What is it?"

"The Indian senses something. Let him take over."

Buxton stared after the disappearing Andrews with the realization that the sergeant was right. Andrews *was* an Indian. Funny he hadn't realized that himself.

"Will he be all right out there alone?" he asked.

Alan grinned. "That man could steal the buttons off your jacket, sir, and you wouldn't know it. Wait."

Gawasowanee wriggled forward, flat against the ground. There had been a sound back there, a sound that he could not identify. Yet it was a manmade sound and he wanted to know more about it.

His right hand slipped his long knife from its scabbard and he carried it now between his teeth. The fog was everywhere. It hid him as it hid the enemy. At any moment he might come face to face with a German and he wanted to be ready.

Then right before him he caught sight of a German helmet. The kraut was looking off to the left, away from him.

Very softly, he gripped the haft of his knife. Then he lifted himself on an elbow and struck right at the neck exposed below the back of that helmet. Deep into the flesh went his steel. The German died without a sound.

Very gently now he lifted off the helmet, gripped the hair, ran his knife around it and ripped. He smiled grimly at the blond scalp in his left hand.

He'd bet the captain's eyes would bulge if he saw that. He slid the scalp into his pocket and moved on.

He was among the trees now. He crawled on, pausing to listen. Faintly he could hear the sound of voices. A tank loomed up in the mists before him. The voices grew louder.

For the first time in his life, Gawasowanee wished he could talk German, or at least, understand it. Not having any idea what the men were saying, he would have to use his eyes. There was armor here, a lot of it. He could tell that by circling slowly and using his eyes when an eddy of breeze shifted the mists. Men were sitting there, smoking cigarettes and chatting.

Gawasowanee moved on, sliding slowly like a snake. Big Snowsnake his people had named him and this day he earned that appellation. He slid here and there. He used his eyes that could almost see through that damn fog.

When he had seen enough, he wriggled out. He went faster now, moving past the body of the sentry he had scalped. He had to report back to that captain what he had seen.

He came up to them, grinning. "They got a helluva lot of tanks and men back there behind the trees. Just waiting, seems like. They're sitting around smoking."

"Any idea when they might attack?" Buxton asked.

"I couldn't understand their talk, sir, but there was one man—an officer, a colonel, I think he was—who kept looking at his watch and at the fog. I got the impression that as soon as the fog lifts, they're coming in at us."

Jim Buxton nodded. This was good enough for him. Without going in among the krauts and asking them personally, he had the answer to what he wanted to know.

Behind them a man cursed in German. Other voices answered them, and in their voices, the men of this patrol could read fear.

"What's bothering them?" Buxton asked.

"This, sir."

Gawasowanee held up the blond scalp he had taken. Captain Buxton stared at it in disbelief.

"You—you *scalped* one of them?"

"Sure did, sir. There's nothing in regulations that says you can't scalp the enemy."

Captain Buxton scowled. The man was right. Think how he could, he could remember nothing in the rule book that said one must not take scalps during the fighting. Slowly his mouth relaxed into a grin. He was remembering Malmedy and the hundred and twenty-five men slaughtered there by the krauts unarmed and with their arms held high.

"You're right, soldier. Carry on. And take all the goddamned kraut scalps you want."

He moved his hand and the patrol started to ease back.

That was when the dozen Germans loomed up out of

the mists. For an instant, nobody moved. Then Gawasowanee yanked his scalping knife and drove it into the belly of the nearest German. He swung aside and thrust those ten inches of cold steel into the next man's throat. The man started at him, eyes wide, even as gouts of blood gushed out.

By this time Max Gluber had shaken off his surprise. His carbine was at his hip and he shot from there, his lips curling back in the hot hatred that gripped him. Then Alan Bishop was firing, and Lou Princezzi.

Before Joe Sullivan could pull his trigger, the Germans were on the ground, dead.

Captain Buxton stared down at them, his hand gripping his automatic pistol. Damn! He should have captured one of them to take back to Headquarters for questioning. A prisoner might have told them a lot.

Sergeant Bishop gripped his wrist and dragged him to the ground. "Lie flat—and still," he grated.

The others were already lying prone.

In a moment, rifle fire tore the air around them. It sang and whistled overhead. Captain Buxton told himself that if it hadn't been for Sergeant Bishop, he might well be a dead man. He would never have thought of return fire.

He glanced sideways at the sergeant. "That was quick thinking. Thanks."

"You get to know what to do almost automatically after a while. I think we'd better get the hell out of here."

They went away as fast as they could crawl. Captain Buxton noted that Andrews was the last man to come and that he would pause as though to listen before he came on after them. This was one damn good unit. He wished they were attached to his command. Hmmm. Maybe he could do something about that when they got back to Headquarters.

After a time they rose to their feet and trotted, shielded by the fog. They could hear no sound but that of their own breathing and the soft plop of their shoes as they trotted on. Momentarily they expected to hear a burst of gunfire from behind them, but none came.

As they neared the stone fence framing the graveyard, a couple of rifles poked forward and Captain Buxton shouted, "Friends, friends. I'm coming in from a patrol."

A hand waved them forward.

As the men with him dispersed to resume their former battle stations. Captain Buxton moved on toward Headquarters. He had done his job, thanks to that Mohawk. He wondered what he would have done if Andrews hadn't been with him.

He would keep an eye on those men. Whenever he had another job to do like that, he wanted them with him. He must remember not to mention that scalp. He didn't know whether the Brass would frown on such a thing, but if they didn't know about it, there wasn't anything they would do.

The day dragged on for Alan Bishop. His belly was empty. It seemed ages since he had last eaten. As he lay behind the stone wall, he remembered the holidays when he had been a youngster in Minnesota and the turkeys that his mother and grandmother had cooked in the big stove. Turkey and stuffing, mashed potatoes, sweet potatoes, peas, all the trimmings, along with cranberry sauce.

His stomach growled at him and he chuckled.

"Don't blame you a bit. It must be hell to be empty and have me thinking about all the other feasts we've had together."

He wondered what the folks were doing, back on the

farm. It was a big dairy farm. They had hundreds of cows and his father had developed a good business. When the war was over, if he lived through it, he would go back to that farm and take over running it. His father was getting on in years, though the old man would have denied it vigorously.

Working on the farm, day in and day out, coming out into those cold Minnesota winter mornings with the breath practically freezing on your lips as you exhaled. That was living. Some of the boys were complaining about how cold it was here. Ha! They should be in Minnesota in mid-winter!

He supposed he would have to find a wife, too, so he could raise some kids to take over the farm after he grew old. There was no special girl for him, thank God. He would hate to be in Lou's shoes with a pretty wife back there in Newark and not being able to do anything about it.

No, he would wait until he saw whether he was going to come out of this war alive before he let himself think about a woman. Well, a woman as a wife, anyhow.

That Matilda Kubek was a woman, all right. She was older than he was, but she had a great figure. Good breasts and a fine pair of hips. Nice legs, too.

Better stop thinking about her though. A man needed to keep his wits unclouded with the krauts readying an assault. He turned his head, looked up and down his men who were crouched behind the stone walls waiting for that attack.

"How's the ammo?" he called.

"Bad, Sarge. Not many rounds left."

They would not be able to get any more ammo either. Not unless the fogs let up so the flyboys could come over and make their drops. Without bullets, they had no way to stop the damned krauts.

Alan Bishop sighed.

Lou Princezzi was dreaming about Maria. She would be writing to him as she did every day, but it had been a long time since he had read one of her letters. It was difficult to get the mail up here to the front lines and now with Bastogne being surrounded, no letters at all would come in.

He had to be satisfied with his memories. Sometimes they weren't enough for a healthy man. And Lou Princezzi felt very healthy. Goddamn! He hated those Germans almost as much as Maxie did.

Paul Andrews felt a prickling down his back. He looked around him, noting that the fog was beginning to lift. He could see things now that had been all but invisible before. He shifted and moved closer to the sergeant.

"It's breaking, Sarge. They'll be coming soon."

"Right. Pass the word."

They waited, alerted, their carbines in their hands, with tommyguns poked forward over the capstones. They were tired and hungry, and in no mood to feel sympathy for any krauts who came walking toward them, expecting to find an easy pushover.

The mists lifted slowly even as a weak, watery sun poured down on them. The tops of the distant trees became visible. Then the men behind the stone fence could make out the ground itself, along which wisps of fog drifted like homeless vagrants.

The sounds of motors roaring came to them, the clank of tank treads beginning. Soon now the mechanized forces of the Second Panzer Division would be battering toward them, seeking to sweep them out of their path.

There was no sound from the men crouched behind the stonework fence or in the foxholes. What need was there of talk? They knew the hell that was gathering out there, the mad fury that would try to brush them off the face of the earth. It was their job to stop that onslaught, to grind it to a halt, to make it retreat.

Overhead they heard the faint hum of planes. Glancing upward they could make out a flight of Messerschmitts. It flew over them bound for some distant target.

Joe Sullivan stared up at those planes for a moment. "If they can get here, why the hell can't ours?"

"They'll come," somebody yelled.

"Yeah, sure—but when?"

Now they could see the tanks coming from the forest, lumbering toward them, moving faster and faster. Where were the Shermans? Where had the tank-destroyers they had disappeared to?

The only sound on that frozen field was the clanking of those tanks. In a short time they would be able to rake the foxholes and the graveyard fence. When they did that—

Alan Bishop sighed. He would never go back to the United States. He would lie here shattered by a shell, one more victim of this goddamn war. He pushed his carbine forward and his face grew grim.

Maybe they would kill him, but he would go out with some krauts. He could make them out, strung along behind the tanks, moving forward foot by foot to add their own fire to that of the Mark IVs.

The whole world erupted right behind him.

He instinctively crouched down as that barrage began. Shells roared along over his head. He saw a big Mark IV explode, sending pieces of itself in every direction. German soldiers, struck by that metal, went down screaming. Another tank was hit, ran lopsidedly for a moment.

Men came pouring out of it.

Alan fired. As he did, he heard the other guns opening up around him. Those men from the tanks took two, maybe three steps on the ground. Then they pitched forward, shot to ribbons.

Now the rifle fire was directed at the foot soldiers, cutting them down. The men were firing sporadically, in bursts, not just for the sake of letting go with their weapons, but with definite targets in mind.

Max Gluber was grinning as he fired.

"Die, you dogs. Die! Die! Die!"

He had never aimed so accurately, as white-clad shape after white-clad shape tumbled to the ground under his fire. There was no thought in his mind except to kill as many men as he could before he himself got killed. He did it coldly, exulting only in a small corner of his being.

Lou Princezzi had lost all memory of his Maria. At this moment he had only one thing in mind: to kill as many krauts as he could before they got him. They were going to kill him, too. Nobody could live through this.

He heard bullets sing overhead, heard the *splaaat* as they they struck the stone wall behind which he was crouched and go screeching off into the air. One of those bullets had his name on it, he was convinced.

Yet he fired, fired, fired. Wherever he saw one of the German soldiers, he sent lead at him. They fell in windrows, lying on that open space before the graveyard fence, sometimes dropping two or three together.

His face was tight, hard. His eyes burned in his head. This was not living, this business of killing men and watching them die out there. This was merely a struggle for survival.

Not me—you! It's your turn to die out there, not mine. Mine will come next, maybe with the bullet that is even now being shot at me—but I'm still alive and while I live I'll go on killing you, as many as I can.

Paul Andrews was unhappy. He would much rather be out there in that open space, grabbing one man and then another, sliding his knife into the flesh of his enemies. But the palefaces did not fight in any such way. No, they stood back and pumped hot lead into their foes.

Well, that hot lead killed just as surely as any knifeblade. That was for sure. He was glad he was not out there in the open, coming on into the rain of bullets that kept mowing down the Germans. Better to be here, protected by this stone wall.

He fired, peered, fired again.

Behind him the Shermans and the tank-destroyers were battering the Mark IVs. They weren't coming on as fast now. Half a dozen of them were in flames out there, lending their reddish light for the men behind the fences and in the foxholes to see by.

One big German tank came on, trying to depress its cannon so as to hit that stone fence and destroy it. Shells roared overhead—damned close. Men instinctively ducked as that big tank poured its fire at them.

"Somebody get that guy," a man screamed.

Then a tank-destroyer fired and its shell hit the German tank in its side, which was not as heavily armored as its front. Something exploded inside the tank. Men could be heard screaming.

Alan Bishop began to pray.

8

It had been a long time since Alan Bishop had prayed. He could not remember the last time, nor the words of any prayer. But he prayed with his whole being, with his mind and his body.

God Above! Get me out of this! Keep me alive. That's all I ask. Just let me live!

His carbine clicked.

Empty!

Oh, this was great. What was he going to do when the krauts came charging in at the fence? He would stand up and use his carbine as a club for as long as he stayed on his feet. Which would not be too long.

"Anybody got any ammo?" he asked hoarsely.

Gawasowanee muttered, "Here, Sarge."

A clip of bullets came flying. Alan caught it, inserted it in his carbine, a wolfish grin on his face.

Now maybe he could stay alive, at least for a little time. He slid the carbine forward and began spraying lead at the oncoming Germans.

Suddenly he stopped firing.

He blinked.

There was nobody out on that field, nothing but smashed tanks and dead bodies. He stared and shook his head. Could it be? Could these battered bastards of his have broken the thrust of the Second Panzer Division?

Joe Sullivan lay slumped behind the wall, gripping his gun. Alan eyed him sharply, crying out, "You hurt,

Joe?"

Joe Sullivan grinned, glancing up at the sergeant. "I'm fine, sarge. I'm just taking a breather. Goddamn, but I'm tired of this shittin' war."

Max Gluber growled, "They ran. The bastards ran."

Lou chuckled hoarsely. "Maxie, I don't think there are enough Germans alive to satisfy you. Or dead, either, for that matter."

"I got three bullets left, I think. Where in hell are the supply boys?"

Alan leaned his helmeted head against the stones of the wall. "They can't get into us, Max, because we're surrounded."

"The sky isn't surrounded. We got airplanes, don't we? What are the generals doing, anyhow? Do they mean for us to die here, like rats in a trap?"

"Hey, that's right. Where are the flyboys? The sky is clear. There's no fog for the first time in about forever. Why aren't they dropping supplies?"

Alan Bishop sighed. "God knows. If we had bullets and food, we could hold off those krauts forever, I think."

"Maybe they've written off Bastogne."

"And us along with it."

Gawasowanee grinned coldly. He had wriggled here and there behind the stone fence, rifling the bodies of dead men, stuffing his pockets with clips of bullets. It had been a good day for him. He had killed at least thirty Germans that he knew about.

He said now, "Good weather now. The planes will come."

Alan turned his head to stare at him. "You mean that, Paulie?"

"Sure. Good weather. Cold but clear, at least for a few days. You listen. You'll hear the planes."

Toward dusk a file of men came sliding toward them. These men appeared fresh. They moved with more pep than anybody in these front lines could summon up. A captain came with them.

"All right, fall out for a time, you guys. We'll take over for you."

Max Gluber growled, "I'll stay here, thanks."

"You got to eat, Max," Lou muttered.

"I got to kill Germans, that's what I got to do. I haven't killed enough of them yet."

"You're crazy, you know that?"

Max only grunted and peered across the body-strewn field toward the distant trees. The krauts would come at them again and he wanted to be here in the front line when they did.

Alan Bishop fell into step beside Paul Andrews. "You heading for the chow line?"

"Not yet. I want to see how Michelle is getting along." The Mohawk drew a deep breath. "The krauts really poured it into Bastogne today. I just hope she's all right."

Alan glanced at him from the corners of his eyes. "She's pretty young, Paul."

The Indian looked surprised. "Of course she's young, just a child. But I feel I got to look in at her, at least."

"Sure. Mind if I walk with you?"

Paul Andrews laughed. "Glad to have you. Been a long time since I've gone calling on anybody that wasn't my own flesh and blood. Funny. I'd never do this back in the States—go calling on a white girl, that is."

"Why not?"

Gawasowanee looked at him. "Where you from, Sarge? Don't you know about such things as the color barrier?"

"Shit. You're a man, a damned good man. That's all

anybody has to know."

"Yeah, yeah. While the fighting's going on. But when it stops? How about then? I'll go back to my own people and help build bigger and better skyscrapers. You'll go back to being a reporter and life will pick up for you just about as it's always been, until the war came along. Me. . .

"Well, I'll go back to my own trade, helping to build skyscrapers. That's one thing they let Indians do, you know." Was that bitterness in his voice? "They know we aren't afraid of heights and so they hire us to put up those steel girders halfway to heaven."

Alan nodded. "You wouldn't catch me up on one of those girders, not for all the gold in Fort Knox."

"It isn't bad. I don't mind it. And the pay is damn good. I've saved my pay. One of these years I intend to buy me a farm in New York State, somewhere up there where the grass grows green and long, and raise me some milk cows. Pigs, too, maybe. And chickens. I'll be able to eat high off the hog for the rest of my life. If I live."

"You have it all figured out."

"Haven't you?"

Alan Bishop thought of Madge Thomas. If Madge had married him, he might have been as anxious as Lou Princezzi to go back home, to be a reporter again. But there was nobody waiting for him on the other side of the Atlantic. Well, there was his family of course, on that Minnesota farm.

He shook his head. "No. Oh, I suppose I'll pick up where I left off, like you. I'll get a job on a paper and write articles for magazines. I used to do that, too, back then. But I'm not looking forward to it."

"You like this war, Sarge?"

"Not the way Maxie does. That's all he lives for, to

kill Germans. In a way I don't blame him. I think he's the only man I know who is truly happy being here in Bastogne with the krauts half a mile away and liable to come at us at any moment."

"Yeah. I've thought about how singleminded he is. A man ought to have more than hate to motivate him though."

They paused as by common consent and stared. They saw where shells from the German guns had ripped into parts of Bastogne. They noted the shattered hulks of buildings that had been homes and offices.

The building in which they had slept last night was still standing unhurt. The houses near it were also unharmed.

Paul Andrews heaved a sigh as relief went through him. "At least, it's still there."

"And your little girl will be safe."

The Mohawk glanced at him. "My little girl?"

"She seems to have adopted you."

"Yeah. Well. . . I don't know whether that's good or bad." He hesitated a moment. "I'm liable to be killed tomorrow, or maybe even tonight."

"And if you're not?" Alan asked quietly.

Gawasowanee only shrugged.

The front door flew open when they were a few feet away from it and Michelle Kubek leaped out, arms widespread, her blue eyes large with delight. She wore a different dress, something that was slightly tight on her so that it revealed the shape of her body.

"My Indian! You came back to me *Le bon Dieu* saved your life for me."

She hurled herself against him and to keep from being knocked backward, Paul Andrews tightened his hold on her. He felt her body against his own, felt all its softness and its curves. Then she was kissing him.

He should not do it, but he kissed her back, knowing an intense pleasure. *This girl is only a child, she is not yet a woman! Be careful, Gawasowanee!* Yet he could not deny the sharp pleasure, the delight, that ran in him.

Alan had walked on toward the door. His back was toward them. The Mohawk hugged her as she drew away her mouth.

"What did you do today?" he asked, breathing hard.

"I prayed for you. What else?"

"Weren't you afraid?"

She smiled up at him and he grew aware that her belly and loins were still pressed close against his own. She was not a tall girl, but neither was he a very tall man. He was six feet, and she was about—oh, say five feet three inches. Yet in that moment he felt she was very much a woman.

"Of course I was afraid," she whispered almost against his lips. "But I prayed, and I felt that God was telling me He would watch over you."

"You're a good pray-er. He certainly did."

"Are you hungry?"

"As a bear."

"Auntie and I have been preparing dinner, hoping you would come."

She caught his hand in hers and drew him into the house. Paul Andrews looked around for his sergeant, but Alan Bishop was nowhere to be seen. Michelle caught his glance and smiled.

"Auntie is entertaining your friend. They will be in the kitchen. You and I shall go out into the garden."

"The garden?"

"Or what is left of it. Those Boches! Their shells fall all over the place. They are awful people."

She brought him along a passageway to a back door and then out into what might once have been a very pleasant garden. There were trellises here and there, covered now by the remnants of flowers that might bloom again in the spring, if the fighting ever stopped. There were neat little paths and banks of what were flowers in the springtime and summer. Now they were only patches of brown color sprinkled with bits of mud.

Michelle pushed him onto a bench, then sat beside him. Her hand held his as she looked at him. "Was it very terrible?" she asked softly.

"Bad enough. But don't talk about the war. Let's talk about you. How do you feel? Have you heard anything about your father and mother?"

Tears came into her eyes and she hung her head.

"No, there has been no news. But I am sure they are dead. I would know, otherwise, in here," and she tapped her heart with a hand. Her eyes grew bigger. "I am all alone in the world, except for Aunt Matilda—and you."

He wanted to tell her that she must not count on him. Sure, he would do all he could for her, as long as he was stationed here. But when the war was over, he was going back to New York. There was nothing to keep him here.

Or—was there?

His eyes roved over her body. She had very good legs. He could see most of them in that short-skirted dress she had on. They were full and shapely. She was shapely all over, come to that. Like a woman in miniature.

Paul sighed. Better get his thoughts off her body. God knows what might happen if he went on looking at her or only thinking about her. He must remember that she was a child. Only fourteen years old.

He wished she wouldn't sit quite so close with her leg and hip against his own. She had put on some perfume, too, probably her aunt's. And now he noticed that she had done up her golden hair so that it coiled high on her head. It made her look older.

"Would you like to take a bath?" she asked suddenly.

"A bath? You mean I can?"

She nodded gleefully. "Oh, yes. The plumbing still works. It may not work tomorrow." Her hand tightened on his. "Come along and I will show you."

He went with her, up the stairway, and to the bathroom. It was a room with a big tub, with a sink and with a toilet bowl. It was in white tile and on the small window there were blue curtains. To Gawasowanee who had been used only to foxholes and dirt, it seemed like something out of heaven.

"Get undressed now and into the tub," she ordered, bending to run the water. As she straightened, she glanced at him. "Take off those dirty clothes. I will wash them for you."

"Hey, you don't have to do that."

Her eyes got big. "I want to."

"All right. I'll throw them out into the hall. Now you just turn around and wait."

He put his hands on her shoulders and marched her to the door. She went reluctantly and Paul Andrews wondered whether she would have stayed to soap him down. Jeez! If she did that, he certainly would not be responsible for what he might do.

When the door was closed, he stripped down and stepped into the bath. The warm water smoothed him and he closed his eyes, leaning back in the tub and just luxuriating.

Ah, this was living. The last time he had had a bath—outside a cold rubdown—had been in England. He had forgotten what creature comforts might be like. He grinned and dreamed a little, lying there, running soap and a washcloth over his big, hard body.

As soon as the war was over, he would have baths like this all the time. He would check into a New York hotel and go at once to the bathtub. He would fill it with hot water and just lie there. Maybe even fall asleep.

Big Snowsnake grinned. Hey, he was in a tub now that was filled with hot water. Enjoy it, man! Forget about when the war ends. Grab at pleasure while you can. You may never go back to New York.

He rubbed and cleansed himself, relishing every moment. He was washing away all the battle-sweat, the tension, the excitement of the past couple of years. Get clean and be a new man. He bent forward to wash his feet, thinking how his socks must absolutely stink.

That was when the door opened and Michelle walked in. Her eyes went to his body and she stared at him.

"Hey! Get out of here!"

She smiled at him, shrugging. "Don't you think I know how a man is made? I was born on a farm and grew up there."

"Yeah, but I wasn't."

A delighted smile curved her mouth. "You are shy! Eh? You do not like to have me in here looking at you, *hein?*

What did a guy do with a girl like this? He couldn't get angry at her, she was so—well, so natural. That was it. She was absolutely natural. She had a feminine curiosity about his body, and so she indulged it by staring at him.

The only trouble with that was, that his body liked her being there and looking at it. A part of him began to react.

Michelle saw it. The water wasn't all that dirty that it could hide him. Her tongue came out to run around her mouth.

"You like me, don't you?" she said softly, nodding her blonde head. "Well, I like you, too."

"Michelle, you're only a kid!"

"I am fourteen, almost fifteen. My mother married my father when she was sixteen. It is done all the time on these farmlands. Why should one wait until she is old, over twenty?"

There was nothing he could say to that.

She bent then and picked up his clothes, wrapping them into a sort of bundle. Paul watched her anxiously. He wouldn't have been surprised if she had taken off her own clothes and climbed in here with him.

At the door, she looked at him. "I will be back to scrub your back for you, my Indian."

Paul opened his mouth to protest, but she was gone, with a little giggle floating back at him. Hell! He had been enjoying himself so much in here. Now he would have to get out and dry himself off and—and wrap a towel around him. There was no way he was going to let her scrub his back.

His eyes roamed the room. There were no towels in here. He blinked and looked again. The minx had probably taken them out before she had brought him in here. She certainly was making sure he stayed in the tub so she could scrub his back for him.

The Mohawk puffed out his lips. Well, now. He was going to have to stay here, all right. She had seen to that. He grinned wryly. That Michelle was some kind of female.

The door opened and she came in, carrying towels. Her eyes danced with delight as she eyed his face.

"So. You couldn't get out, could you? I am a good thinker. I look ahead. I anticipate." She grinned at him.

Paul laughed. "Okay, okay. So scrub my back."

She bent to her task with a smile, washing his back

and scrubbing it with a brush. She scrubbed so hard at times that he muttered under his breath.

"Do I hurt?" she asked softly.

"A little."

Now her hands came on his flesh to rub the soap over it. Gawasowanee decided that it might be better if she used the brush. Those soft hands going over him were too exciting. To his surprise when she had finished and poured water over his back from a little pail, she turned toward the door.

"Your clothes are soaking," she told him. "You will have to wrap yourself in a towel and wait in the bedroom."

He eyed her warily. "How long?"

She stuck her tongue out. "Until I can go get some of Uncle Derek's clothes. They may fit you. He was a big man."

"Was?"

Her eyes filled with tears. "He is dead. He died a few weeks ago. No, the Germans did not kill him. He caught a cold, and died. I will miss him. He was a good man, always cheerful, always laughing."

There was a sob in her voice. She brushed a hand across her eyes and swung away, opening the door and going out. Paul sat there in the tub, thinking.

The poor kid. She had no immediate family and only an aunt. How the hell was she going to make it when the war ended? Well, she had a farm, or what was left of one. Could a girl of her age run a farm?

It occurred to him that he understood farming. He had been born and brought up on a farm in upper New York State. Why, when he got through with this war, he planned to start a farm of his own up near the Adirondacks. If he brought Michelle and her aunt back with him. . . .

Ah, that was nonsense. They wouldn't want to leave their homeland. He ran the towels over his big body thoughtfully. Then he wrapped the largest one around him and went out into the hall, heading toward the bedroom where he had slept last night.

He could smell meat cooking and it came to him that he was damn near starved. It had been a long time since he had eaten breakfast in this house.

He wondered where the sergeant was and what he was doing.

Alan Bishop was in the kitchen, peeling potatoes. There was a big apron around him and the smell of roasting meat was in his nostrils.

As soon as he had entered the kitchen, Matilda Kubek had turned to him with a big smile. There was flour on her hands and forearms and a sprinkle of it across her nose where she must have scratched.

"You are alive," she had whispered, the delight at seeing him glowing in her brown eyes.

"And I'm here to help you prepare dinner."

"You? What does a man know about cooking?"

He laughed. "A lot. I'll show you. What's in the oven, roast beef? Jeez, I haven't tasted good roast beef in I don't know how long. You got any potatoes and onions?"

She nodded slowly, eyes dancing. "And what are you going to do with potatoes and onions?"

"Make some hash browns. I haven't had those in a ton of years."

She eyed him a moment, then shrugged. "Very well. I do not know what these 'ash browns are, but I am willing to try."

When he had the onions before him, he began slicing them. Matilda laughed to see the tears streaming down his cheeks. He grinned in answer to that laughter, liking this woman and her warm ways.

Now he sliced the potatoes and mixed them and the onions in a big frying pan. He turned them slowly, his mouth watering to their smell. Matilda stood at his elbow, staring down into the pan.

She said, "If they taste half as good as they smell, they will be delicious."

"They will." He hesitated a moment, then murmured, "Your niece is an orphan, isn't she?"

"I am afraid so. Her family is gone, all killed by the Germans."

"Will she stay with you when the war is over?"

"There is a big farm out there which will belong to her. Once it was a very fine farm, but now," she shrugged, "the Germans will have killed all the animals and eaten them, I am afraid. There isn't much left for her to go home to, just the house and the barns and the outbuildings."

Her eyes lifted from the big skillet. "Why do you ask?"

"She's pretty chummy with the Mohawk."

Her brown eyes looked worried. "He is not a good man?"

"The best," Alan hastened to assure her. "I'd trust him with my life."

"And with your daughter's virtue?"

He hesitated. Then he chuckled. "Yes, even that. But war does funny things to people. It tends to lower their morals, if not their morale. A lot of children are born at wartime—nature's way of making certain the race goes on."

"I have not noticed," she murmured wryly.

Alan glanced at her sharply. Was she hinting? Yet her face was not provocative. She was not moving close to him. Still, he began to wonder.

Now he eyed her in a new light. She was not as old as he had thought the first time he had seen her. The lines seemed to have disappeared from her face and her clothes were smarter, neater. There had been a period of mourning for her husband. Maybe that had affected her.

She might be his own age.

He would have to find out.

9

Paul Andrews was standing at a window, wearing only the big towel, when Michelle came into the room. She carried his uniform, hurriedly cleaned and brushed. Her blue eyes laughed at the sight of him.

"I have cleaned this up as best I could," she smiled, holding out his clothes. "You'd better get into them fast. My aunt says supper will be ready in a few minutes."

He nodded, watching as she put the uniform down on the bed and moved toward the door. For some reason she seemed older than her fourteen years at the moment. Maybe it was the way she walked, or it might be that manner she had of looking at him.

He dressed slowly, thinking. If he were to stay here tonight and sleep in this bed, and if she were to come in and sleep with him. . . .

No. He had to remember she was still a kid.

Gawasowanee made a face. Damned if he would let her climb into that bed with him. He wasn't made of stone, he had feelings. He had repressed his body this morning. He doubted that he could do it again tonight.

When he was fully clad, he went downstairs.

They were eating when they heard the drone of airplane engines. The planes were far away at first, but they were coming closer, closer.

The Mohawk heard them first, lifting his head so suddenly that the others stared at him. "Planes," he whispered.

Alan Bishop asked, "Ours?"

Paul shook his head. "I can't tell, not yet. But I don't think so. They sound German."

Matilda Kubek whispered a prayer, crossing herself. "If it is the Luftwaffe, they will have Bastogne for a target. They will bomb us!"

There was a hysterical note in her voice.

Michelle licked her lips, her eyes fastened on the Indian. She was terrified inside. She still remembered the day the Boches had come to the farm and had shot down her father and mother. She had fled and they had not bothered to go after her. Yet the sound of those rifles was still in her memory.

"What shall we do?" she whispered.

They all heard the planes now. Alan got to his feet, reaching out a hand toward the widow. "Come on. Into the cellar, all of us. It's the safest place."

"My dinner," wailed Matilda.

"Grab your plates, everything you can carry," Paul yelled.

They heard the anti-aircraft guns sounding as they ran. The thunder of the airplain motors was almost deafening and then they heard a bomb hit, somewhere out on the edge of the town. They fled down the stairs, huddled together near a window.

"Sit down," Alan told them. "Eat. Try to act as normally as possible."

"How can one act normally at a time like this?" asked a frightened Matilda, staring up at him.

"I know, I know. But—"

A bomb exploding nearby shook the house. Glass tinkled, off somewhere close. Another bomb fell and another. The rattle of the anti-aircraft guns was incessant. The house itself seemed to shudder and shake and its timbers groaned.

"Where in hell are our own flyboys?" Paul grated. "If the Luftwafe can use the skies, why can't they? Doesn't anybody in this man's army give a damn about Bastogne?"

He crouched close to the cellar wall, discovering that Michelle was pressing herself against him as tightly as she could. He put his arms around her and held her. Her head was nestled on his chest, just under his chin and he could smell the perfume of that long blonde hair.

The bombing went on, seemingly forever.

The house shuddered again and again, its timbers protesting the strain. But so far not a bomb had fallen on it. That luck wouldn't hold, it couldn't hold, the Mohawk kept telling himself. Sooner or later one of those big babies was going to come through the roof and explode, and when it did. . . .

He held Michelle tighter, his hands spread on her back. She was soft and warm to his touch. She huddled against him as though safety were nowhere else. Over her head he could make out—but only dimly—the shapes of the sergeant and Matilda Kubek.

They were pressed together much as he and the girl were, though they were on the opposite wall, seated on the floor, their arms about each other. They seemed to be turned to stone, unmoving.

"You'll be all right," he found himself whispering into her hair. "Nothing will hurt you."

She lifted her head and stared into his eyes. She was very close, there were not more than two inches between his lips and hers.

"I am not afraid for myself," she whispered back. "It is you I worry about."

"Me?"

She nodded. "Yes. You have to go out and fight some more tomorrow and the next day. And if you live, the day after that. I am frightened that—that you will be killed."

His arm tightened about her. Seemingly of its own volition. That brought her in closer. They her lips were on his, kissing him hard.

Gawasowanee told himself that he ought to push her away. She was too young, a child. And yet—and yet—there was a maturity about her that would not have been evident in an American girl. It was not a matter of her body size, but of her mind and her emotions.

"I won't be killed," he told her. "I'm going to stay alive, just for you.

She pressed her cheek against his. "When the war is over, I will have a fine, big farm." She hesitated. "Do you know anything about farming?"

"Sure. I was born on a farm and grew up on it."

Delight exploded across her face. "Really?"

"I've milked more cows and sheared more sheep that you can count."

She nestled against him. "I will not be able to work my farm all by myself," she murmured in a low voice.

"We'll have to talk about that, just as soon as the war is over."

She gave a little sigh and her eyelids closed.

It was dark in the cellar. Gawasowanee could not see across it to where Alan Bishop held Matilda Kubek in his arms.

Alan was only too well aware of the widow woman. Her breasts made soft mounds against his chest as he held her tight to him against the thud and thunder of the bombs. Her thigh was pressed to his and her arm was about his neck.

"We may die here this night," she whispered once.

"Everybody has to die sometime."

Her arm tightened around his neck. "But to go like

this, like frightened rats. . . ."

Alan lifted his head. There was silence all around them. No more bombs were falling. Was the attack over? Had the krauts dropped their loads and flown away? Could it be? Were they alive? Were they going to live?

Excitement worked in him. He looked down at the woman he held. He could see the tip of her nose, the curve of a cheek.

"I think it's over," he murmured.

She glanced up at him. Their eyes locked.

His arm drew her up to him so he could feel both her breasts against his chest. Her mouth was dark, inviting. Alan bent his head and kissed her. Hungrily. Against his chest, he felt her breasts harden.

She wanted him then as much as he wanted her. He strained her against him, his hands sliding down her back and toward her buttocks. Those buttocks were soft, curving.

When she drew away, as though to breathe, he murmured, "I want you. Desperately."

By the faint light in the cellar, he knew she was smiling. "Do you not realize I want you as well? Come! We will go upstairs together."

Alan hesitated. "What about your niece?"

Matilda was standing, holding his head as though to lift him upward. "She is a big girl now. Besides she likes that man she is with very much."

Alan shook his head. Maybe he ought to object, or give Paul some advice. But hell! The Mohawk was a grown man. He knew the score. If he wanted the girl and she wanted him, what did it matter? They might all be dead two days from now.

He went up the cellar stairs with Matilda ahead of him. It was dark, but there was a moon shining and when they passed a window on the first floor, he saw that everything seemed ghostly.

Outside was silence. Nothing moved. For all he knew Bastogne no longer existed, save for this house. And it was cold. Winter was a day or so away, but already it was sending its chill before it.

They moved up the stairs and into a room.

Matilda scratched a match, lighted a candle. She went to a window and drew the drapes. Then she moved to the other window. After the drapes were closed, she turned and smiled at him.

"I was a faithful wife, as long as my husband lived."

Alan smiled. "I'll be gentle."

"Ah, bah. I do not care if you are rough. I am not made of glass, to break at a touch."

Her hands went to the buttons on her dress.

In the cellar Michelle stirred, lifting her head from the Mohawk's chest. She stared into his face, murmuring, "It is so quiet. As if the whole world had died."

"That's because the Luftwaffe flew away. They dumped their bombs and left."

"Then let's go to bed."

She said it so simply, as though they were married, that Paul merely nodded. Not until he was standing and starting to follow her, did he realize that the sergeant and Michelle's aunt were not with them. He pulled back on the hand that held his, halting her.

"Look," he said softly, "you're just a kid. If you think I'm going to sleep with you tonight, you're crazy."

Her face seemed to crumple even as her blue eyes searched deep into his. "You do not like me?" she asked brokenly.

"Of course I like you. Don't be silly."

She smiled up at him radiantly. "That is good,

because I like you, very much. I think I am—in love with you."

Gawasowanee groaned. "You're just a child!"

To his consternation, she moved closer, crowding her body in against him. He felt her thighs, her belly, and against his will, his flesh reacted to that touching. She leaned up, standing on tiptoe and bit his chin, very gently.

He put his arms around her, almost as a reflex action. And that was a mistake, because it brought her in even closer. She began to wriggle a little, caressing his body with her own.

"You're a little devil," he whispered.

"But you like me."

"Sure I like you. Very much. But you're too young."

He had to keep telling himself that, Paul thought. Over and over again, without stop. Because if he didn't, his own flesh would take command of himself and before he knew it, he would be in that bed with this kid and then—well, it would be too late, that's all.

"Ah, pouff! What do you know about too young or not too young? Come with me. I will show you."

Paul Andrews sighed. What could he do with a girl like this? He ought to count himself lucky. The rest of the 101st Aurborne, the Five-O-Sinks, the 705th Tank Destroyer Battalion, all the other men who were here in Bastogne were out there in the cold.

Nobody had a girl like this to share his bed.

Besides, he could always marry her.

He went up the stairs with his arm about her middle. He felt her hip and leg moving with his own and he told himself that this was destiny, the doing of those spirits his people called the Honochenakeh.

So be it then.

She brought him up the stairs—they crept silently,

like conspirators—and then they were in her room and she was closing the door very softly. She looked at him and waited.

He crossed the open space between them and put his hands on her shoulders. His fingers tightened, though not enough to hurt her. His eyes bored down into hers.

"Will you marry me?" he asked softly. "I mean, when this war is over and we can go back to being people again?"

Her laughter was soft, intimate. It seemed to wrap itself about him. "Certainly I will marry you, my big Indian. With you as my husband, we can run my farm and make it as it once was, the finest anywhere about."

She hesitated. "You do not have anyone in your home country to return to? No—sweetheart?"

"No sweetheart," he grinned.

She flung herself against him with a little cry. He felt the softness of her body, the eager pressure of her thighs and belly. His arms went about her and held her against him.

I should not be doing this. She is just a child! But she is so sweet, so innocent, so much everything I have always dreamed a girl should be!

He kissed her, gently at first, aware of the soft opening of her lips and then the fervid thrusting of her tongue. Paul Andrews was a little surprised. Maybe these European girls matured faster than did the girls of his own people. No Mohawk girl would behave in such a way. Or—would she? Gawasowanee admitted to himself that he did not know.

She felt his arousal and moved against it with her leg. Paul told himself to go easy. He did not want to shock her or scare her. He held her tightly, he kissed her and his hands wandered a little over her back, her buttocks.

What might have happened then, he never knew.

Because at that instant, as he was thinking about lifting her and carrying her toward the bed, there was a drone of airplanes.

Instinctively they broke apart, staring into each other's eyes. "Another attack," Michelle whispered.

"Down into the cellar," he nodded.

They were out in the hall and moving toward the stairs when the drone of the planes began to recede. They halted and stared upward at the ceiling, instinctively. Frozen for the moment, they listened.

Soon the planes were gone. Gawasowanee did not know whether they had been German or American. It did not matter, really. The spell between them was broken.

He said, "You aren't going to sleep with me tonight. We're going to wait until this damned war is over and then we're going to be married. You understand?"

Her eyes seemed to glow as she looked up at him. There was a wistfulness about her that touched him deeply. "You love me so much?" she whispered.

"Even more," he grinned, kissing the tip of her nose.

She frowned, thinking. Then she nodded. "Very well. It will be as you say. I will sleeep in another room." She sighed. "Though I do not want to, you know."

"Nor do I. But it must be."

"I suppose so." She grinned wickedly. "You want a virgin bride."

"It isn't that at all."

"Then what?"

"If I should get killed and you were to have a child of mine. . . ."

"I would not care! Pouff! What difference would it make? I would love him—or her—for your sake."

He smiled down at her, drawing her close and kissing her forehead. "When you have a child by me, I want to be there to share the experience."

Michelle nodded soberly. "Yes. I like that. Then come. You shall go back to your bed and I shall go to mine. We will behave ourselves, *hein*? And I shall pray very hard that the good Lord will spare you in the fighting that is ahead."

She caught his hand and drew him back along the hall.

Max Gluber stirred restlessly in his sleep. His dream concerned the old days in Germany, before he had left that country to seek asylum in the United States, and in that dream, his father and mother were still alive.

They were seated at the table enjoying a meal. His younger sister was there with them and she was laughing, telling them of an experience she had had in school. Max was smiling at her tale, but inwardly he was crying.

Somehow he knew that they were all going to die. They were going to be taken to Buchenwald, along with cousins and friends, all of them Jews, and they were going to be put into the gas ovens. He could not help it, he began to cry. The worst of it was, no one noticed. It was as though he were invisible.

He woke, sobbing softly.

His eyes, tear-dimmed, opened on dawnlight. He lay a moment on the ground, wrapped in his big overcoat, and shivered.

"Mama, Papa, Louise," he whispered.

He made a fist of his big hand and shook it in the air. If he had not left his family to go to the United States, he too would be dead. Oh, he might have fought the Nazis when their SS men came to arrest him and his family. If he had, they would have beaten him with clubs until he was all bloody and unable to resist any more.

No, it was better that he had run away.

The Americans had a saying about that. Run away today and fight another day. Yes. Well, he was back now, and he was fighting. But no matter how much he fought, he never seemed to be able to kill enough Germans to satisfy himself.

He grinned mirthlessly. He was in a good position to kill Nazis anyhow. They would be coming at Bastogne in a few hours, along with their big Mark IV tanks.

He would get his chance.

A movement off to one side caught his eye. Lou Princezzi was stirring, sitting up, staring around him. The Italian-American groaned. He had been dreaming of his Maria.

"Goddamn this war," he muttered.

"The war is good," Max muttered. "It is the Germans you should be Goddamning."

"Them, too," agreed Lou, getting to his feet and stretching. He thought a moment. "Especially them."

They looked down at Joe Sullivan who was still asleep. His body was curled up almost in the fetal position and there was a deep peace on his thin face. He never stirred, he was sunk in slumber.

"Probably knocking some guy out in the ring," Lou grunted.

Max sighed. "The war has interrupted his career. It is too bad. He will never become a champion now. He will be too old."

Lou glanced at him. "You mean he won't have a job when he goes back to the States?"

"What sort of job? Maybe a bricklayer or a steamfitter, if he knows anything about those trades. But his life's dream—ah, that will be gone forever."

"Maybe he could teach boxing somewhere. You

know, at a college."

"It could be. If he lives."

"If any of us live," Lou nodded glumly.

Max smiled gently. "You are hungry, my friend. I heard talk last night that there would be flapjacks for breakfast with hot coffee."

"Ersatz coffee, not the real thing."

"What's the diference? It will fill our bellies and help keep us warm."

They trudged off side by side. It was beginning to snow again, though not heavily.

Joe Sullivan wanted never to move. He had awakened from a dream in which he was pounding the world champion into insensibility, driving him back and back into the ropes. Every time he swung an arm, his fist connected. There was exultation inside him, he was going to be the next light heavyweight champion of the world. He could taste it in his mouth.

Just another uppercut or two and the champion would slide down onto that canvas for the count.

But it was cold. Even as he fought, he was aware of the chill seeping all through him. How could they expect a man to fight for the championship when there was no heat in the ring? Just as soon as this fight was over and he was World Champion, he was going to lodge a protest.

He opened his eyes. He saw the shell-torn side of a building and the huddled bodies of men in uniforms. Joe Sullivan closed his eyes and groaned. That dream had been so real! His hands ached from the pounding he had given that guy in the ring. No, it wasn't from the pounding but from the cold.

He lifted his hands and blew on them, though it did little good. He might as well go and get some chow. Maybe that would warm him.

Wearily he picked up his carbine and began his walk.

Damn this war. It robbed a man of everything. He had begun to feel like Max lately. He hated the Germans almost as much as did Gluber. The Germans not only killed Max's family, they had also deprived him of the shot at that championship. Max was right.

No prisoners. Kill the goddamn krauts.

He walked on.

10

Alan Bishop woke to warmth and the awareness of a naked body against his own. It was a soft body. He lay a moment, eyes closed, remembering.

She had been sweet and warm and loving, this woman who lay beside him, last night. She had come to him with a smile on her full mouth and helped him to undress, even while she had been fully clothed.

Her hand had touched his male flesh, found it rigid with need. Her eyes had warmed at the sight. There had been a faint flush on her cheeks, and when he had put his hands to her dress, she had let him strip her down.

Matilda Kubek possessed a fabulous body. Her breasts were full, heavy, though they stood up firmly and their brown nipples pointed right at him. Her belly was smooth, unwrinkled, and her legs were as good as those of Betty Grable. There was a thatch of brown pubic hair on her mons veneris.

She smiled gleefully as his eyes went over her and she struck a pose. "Well? Will I do?"

Alan grinned. "It's been a long time for me. A long time. I have to get to know how a woman is made, all over again."

She grew sober. "And for me. My husband died some time ago, but before that he was a sick man. We did not have relations. I have almost forgotten how it can be."

Alan nodded and moved toward her, putting his arms about her and drawing her in against him. It was good to feel a woman's nakedness, it made him want to yell in delight. For so long a time, he had been slogging through mud or dropping out of the sky, or just standing and fighting, that it seemed to him that something like this was merely a pleasant dream.

Yet the fury in his blood and in his stiffened flesh told him this was life. He was here with a naked woman in his arms and there was a bed just a few feet away. Her arms were around his neck and she was moving her belly and thighs against him.

He kissed her hungrily, mouth open, his tongue seeking out her own. She moaned, pushing against him, her arms gripping him as though she were afraid he would vanish into thin air. Their bodies slithered together. He felt himself gripped by her soft thighs.

"You will not hurry?" she whispered, looking up into his eyes. "You will take your time?"

"I want that even more than you do."

He had made love to her slowly, gently. There was not an inch of her superb body he had not kissed. She had moaned and quivered, trembling in the ecstacy of what he was doing to her, and when she had opened her thighs to take him, they had wallowed in that pleasure of the senses which the French name 'the little death.'

And now it was morning.

Alan stared down into her face. It was a beautiful face, really, and he was surprised at himself that he had never noticed her beauty. There was a calmness, a quietness about her that was deceiving. Matilda Kubek was not a woman given to emotional storms—except perhaps in bed with a man she liked. She had been something, all right.

Her eyes opened and she whispered, looking into his eyes, "What are you thinking?"

"I was remembering last night. I have never experienced anything like it."

Her eyes widened. "You were not a virgin, surely?"

"No. I never met the right woman, I guess. Until now."

What made him say that? It was almost like a proposal of marriage. Still, he could do worse than marry this woman. He put his hands on her nakedness, beneath the covers, fondling her hip and thigh.

She smiled at him. It was a good smile, friendly and warm. It told him that she admired him as a lover, as a man. A warmth blossomed inside Alan Bishop.

"You like to touch me," she whispered.

"Do you mind?"

Her laughter was soft, subdued, but there was a note of wantonness in it. "Certainly not! What sort of woman do you think I am?"

He was remembering Madge Thomas. She had gone to bed with him eagerly enough, but in the morning there had been no closeness between them. It appeared that she couldn't get out of bed fast enough.

He liked lying here naked with this woman naked beside him. All too soon he was going to have to get out of bed and into his uniform and go back to fighting a war, to the sound of gunfire and the screams of men shot and wounded, dying in agony.

"I never thought a woman like you lived," he told her, drawing her even closer so he could kiss her mouth.

He lingered over her mouth for several minutes, enjoying its softness, the moisture of her tongue. He was getting hot again, and the pressure of her big breasts on his chest was adding to his pleasure.

His hands caressed her breasts. She moved back slightly to give them room. Her eyes were like pools of brown fire. When he caught her nipples between his forefingers and thumbs to rotate them, she breathed more quickly and her legs stirred.

Alan bent and kissed those breasts. He drew their nipples into his mouth and suckled. Above his down-bent head, Matilda Kubek moaned softly.

Her arms came forward and drew him to her.

Gawasowanee slept on. In his dreams he wandered the northland woods with a rifle in his hands, seeking for a deer. He saw one between the trees, but his arms would not lift the Winchester. The deer turned and saw him, but instead of running away, it moved toward him and began to nuzzle his cheek.

The deer began to giggle.

That was when Paul Andrews opened his eyes to discover Michelle kneeling on the bed, bending over him, nuzzling his cheek and throat.

"You are a sleepy one," she laughed. "You'd better get up now and get dressed. There are soldiers out in the streets, all moving in one direction. I would not want them to think you are a deserter."

"Jeez, no. They shoot deserters."

He was wearing shorts, so he slid out of bed and moved toward his uniform. The girl sat on the edge of the bed and watched him interestedly.

"I have cooked breakfast for you and the sergeant. I am not calling him yet. He and my aunt are making love." She giggled. "I heard them when I went past the door."

"Oh, my God," he whispered.

She looked surprised. "You are not shocked, are you? My aunt is a lonely woman. Your sergeant is a lonely man. It is good for them to enjoy each other. Don't you think so?"

He nodded. Hell, why not? There was little enough pleasure in this war. A guy deserved whatever pleasure he could find. He himself was a damn fool not to have taken Michelle into his bed last night.

But as he pulled on his pants and looked at her, he knew he had made no mistake. This was a girl he wanted as his wife. In Belgium there would be no prejudice against him because of his red skin. It was something to keep in mind.

He was dressed, then, and he said, "How about that breakfast? I could eat a horse."

She smiled and came off the bed, walking toward him. He put his arms about her and held her close, kissing her forehead, her nose, and finally her mouth. She urged her body against him.

When he let her go, she said, "I like the way you hold me and kiss me."

"I'll do more than that when this war is over."

Her eyes widened, filling with glee. "You will be my husband, then, yes? You will not get tired of me, will you? And go chasing after other women?"

"I have the feeling you'll keep me too busy loving you to bother about other women."

She nodded thoughtfully. "Yes. That is exactly what I shall do. Between me and the farm, you will be kept too busy to think about anything else."

Well, that was fine by him. Just let him live long enough to marry her and he would prove that to be true.

They tiptoed down the stairs, carefully avoiding Aunt Matilda's bedroom door and the sounds that might be coming from the bed.

Paul went to a window and stared out at the troops moving along the street. He supposed he and the sarge ought to be out there, but he wasn't going to leave here until he had had his breakfast. If the sarge missed it, that was his hard luck.

The smell of frying bacon swung him around. He went into the kitchen where Michelle was standing before the stove, turning over strips of bacon in the big skillet. She made a pretty picture standing there, with her long blonde hair and her dress clinging to her body. The sight of her made him realize how much he wanted her, how much he needed to come back alive out of this fighting.

She turned and her blue eyes touched his. "It will be ready soon. You will have to join your troops, I know. But for the moment, you can relax."

He went to her and caught her in his arms. There was delighted surprise in her face and she pressed herself against him even as he kissed her hungrily.

"I'll come back to you," he whispered. "I promise it."

She nodded, smiling wanly. "I hope so. I pray that you will, all the time."

Michelle smiled then and pushed him away. "Go sit down. How can I cook when you are tempting me so much?"

Paul grinned and moved away, hearing Alan Bishop and Matilda Kubek coming down the stairs. In a moment they were with them in the kitchen.

They ate breakfast together, not saying much and not smiling, with worry in the eyes of the women and a grimness about the men. Michelle stood up when it was over and walked into the next room. Paul picked up his carbine and went after her.

Matilda said softly, "Come back to me, Alan. I will be waiting."

He nodded soberly. "If I can, I will."

She put out her hand and he caught it, squeezing. Then he got up and followed after the Indian. Paul was waiting beside the door, Michelle standing close to him.

"Let's go," Alan muttered, and opened the door.

They walked out into the stream of troops moving through the town, fell into step with them, looking for the others of their platoon.

"What's the word?" Alan asked a man walking beside him.

"The krauts are attacking us to the south. We're moving up to stop them."

"The south?"

The man grinned. "We beat the shit out of them when they came at us from the east, so they've changed their tactics. A whole Panzer division is headed this way, meaning to overrun the place, I guess. It's our job to stop 'em."

"We got any support?"

"Hell, yes. The bazooka boys and the heavy stuff are waiting for them. The krauts don't know it, but we'll be ready for 'em."

They were moving out of town when a voice hailed them and Max Gluber, Lou Princezzi and Joe Sullivan came up to them.

Joe said, "No need to ask where you two were last night."

Max grunted, "No need. Now we're on the move again."

Alan said, "You could have come with us."

Lou Princezzi chuckled. "We had the feeling we might be in the way."

They tramped on. The snow had stopped long ago, but it glittered in the rays of the weak sunlight on the fields toward which they moved. The sky was clear, its blueness containing only a few clouds. It was a good day for dying, the Mohawk was telling himself. The only trouble was, he did not intend to die, not if he could help it.

They fanned out after a time and began to dig foxholes. The Germans were somewhere out there waiting. In a little while they would throw themselves at these few defenders of Bastogne. They would fill the blue skies with shells that would come in *cruuump cruuump* and when they hit there would be nothing but a hole.

Lou Princezzi made his foxhole with the ease of long practice. He got down into it, his carbine facing toward the south. He began to pray. It had been a long time since he had prayed, longer than he cared to remember, he thought uneasily. Once he had been an altar boy at the church where his family had worshipped in Newark and he guessed he had been as good an altar boy as there had been.

Oh, sure. He got into fights every so often, but what boy didn't? It was fists then, not guns. He had always held his own, though he had not gone looking for trouble as some of his friends had done.

He snuggled closer to the dirt of his foxhole, peering ahead of him. Nothing yet. He could go back to dreaming for a little while and remember Maria as she had been on that morning—What had it been? The second or third day of their honeymoon?—when she had walked naked around the hotel room and let him look at her.

Jeez! If only he were with her now. She wouldn't do much walking, that was for sure. She would be flat on her back and he would be with her, proving to her how much he loved her. He lost himself in his reveries.

Joe Sullivan was sharing his foxhole with a man from the Five-O-Deuce outfit, a big man with a weather-beaten face and a lanky frame. This man was quiet, but once he glanced at Sullivan and grinned slightly.

"You know what the guys are calling us?" he asked suddenly.

Joe looked at him. "No. What?"

"The battered bastards of Bastogne." The lanky man

chuckled. "Pretty good, huh? Goddamn if I don't feel like a battered bastard, right about now."

Joe grinned. "The battered bastards. Hey, that's good. I like it."

He called over to the next foxhole. "Hey, Sarge, they're calling us the battered bastards of Bastogne."

Alan smiled tightly. "That's what we are, all right. And we're going to get battered a lot more pretty soon. Listen!"

They could hear it now, the low drone of heavy airplaine motors. The sound filled the air. It grew louder and louder. Some of the men in the foxholes cursed and lay even flatter to the ground. Out here in the open, they were sitting ducks for an air attack.

Then somebody yelled, "Hey, they're ours!"

They could make them out now: big C-47s carrying the much needed ammunition and supplies. German anti-aircraft batteries went to work and soon the air around the planes was filled with the white clouds of shellbursts. The C-47s flew on.

Now they began to dump their loads.

Parachutes blossomed outward like expanding flowers. The sky above seemed filled with them. Here and there the men in the foxholes began to cheer. With enough ammo they could hold off those krauts until Kingdom Come.

Apparently the Germans felt much the same way because almost instantly they launched their attack. The big Mark IVs began lumbering forward, followed by the foot soldiers. The men in the foxholes forgot about the C-47s. They had more serious things to keep them busy.

Max Gluber was happy. He could make out the forms of Germans coming toward him. He lay in his foxhole and he poked his carbine out, facing the oncoming wave of men and metal. He waited, not being a man to waste his bullets. When he fired, he wanted to be sure of the result.

The Mark IVs began dropping shells.

Max hunched down, his eyes slitted, watching the enemy foot soldiers. They were his concern. He would leave the tanks to the bazooka men and to the Tank Destroyers. In a few moments he heard them both opening up.

A German tank burst into flames. Max grinned. *Cook, you sons-of-bitches! I hope the fire in that tank is like a foretaste of Hell!* His hands tightened on the carbine. The red flames from that tank gave good light to shoot by.

He began to fire.

A burst and then a rest, another burst and another rest. He saw the krauts drop before his gunfire and exultation came alive in him. Kill as many as he could, then kill some more. None of them deserved to live.

This war, this battle, was his own personal crusade against Germany. Fire up their gas ovens, would they? Kill his family and the families of other Jews? They would pay for those horrors, here and now.

He shot carefully, as was his habit. He ignored the shells bursting around him, ignored the scream of the shrapnel that whistled through the air. If it was his turn to be wounded or killed, then he would be. But until something put him out of commission, he would go on killing.

Off to one side of him, Joe Sullivan was also firing. Though he was not quite as bitter as was Max Gluber, yet he felt inside him a sense of resentment against the krauts. If it hadn't been for them and this Goddamned war they had started, he might be champion of the world.

They had wanted a war. Well, now they had one.

How did they like it, the bastards? It wasn't all peaches and cream any more, no more overrunning of France and Russia as they had done in the first year or two of the war. Now the Allies were fighting back, throwing everything they had at the krauts.

Another big German tank exploded, and then another. The foot soldiers behind those tanks came on stubbornly, only to be mowed down by the fire from the foxholes.

Alan Bishop was shooting as carefully as Max Gluber. He had no hatred of the Germans such as Max did, but he knew they were the enemy, out there to kill him if they could. As somebody had said, the best defense is a good offense.

If you could kill enough Germans, the war would end. Alan set himself to killing them.

Beside him in the foxhole, Paul Andrews also shot to kill. He did it cooly, methodically, but with only half his mind. He kept thinking about Michelle Kubek, remembering the softness of her body and the sweetness of her mouth when she had kissed him.

He meant to live, to go back to her. The best way to do that was to get rid of the men who would kill him and prevent it. Gawasowanee would have preferred to be fighting in a different way. He would have preferred sliding forward on his belly under cover of night with his knife between his teeth, but this way was closed to him at the moment.

Oh, well. Shooting krauts from this foxhole was serving the same purpose. If only it weren't so cold! His fingers and toes seemed frozen and he would have to blow air from his lungs at his fingers every so often to keep them working effectively. There wasn't anything he could do about his toes, however.

He saw five Germans running toward him. They

seemed to have sprung up out of nowhere. Their rifles were firing, but their bullets were going high.

"You belong to me, you bastards," he whispered through his teeth, and began to fire.

The five went down as though mowed by a huge scythe. The Mohawk eyed them a moment, then decided they would give no more trouble to anyone.

They fought on, turning back the repeated German thrusts at their positions. Here and there men were screaming in agony, but they closed their ears to those screams as best they could. It might be their turn to be yelling like that next.

A tank-destroyer came toward them, easing forward between the foxholes in an attempt to get closer to the tanks as they lumbered at the foxholes. A moment it paused and then its big cannon began to boom.

Lou Princezzi watched as a Mark IV exploded. He saw another one whirl and turn as though to take care of this audacious enemy. But the shell from the tank-destroyer caught the German tank before it could complete its turn. Its shell hit its side. There was a red flower of fire and exploding metal and then screams lifted into the air.

Lou shuddered, picturing the plight of the Germans trapped inside that tank. Christ! What a way to die! He wanted to leap to his feet, to shout out and stop all this killing, but he knew this was only hysteria blossoming inside him.

Better get back to killing. That way he would be concentrating on something he knew how to do. He lifted his carbine and sent a stream of bullets toward the wavering line of white-clad Germans behind those tanks.

How long was this going to go on? They had been here for an eternity, it seemed, though it was only about four or five days. Yet in that short space of time, they had been through hell, had come back, and then gone into hell again.

His eyes scanned the snowy fields before him. German dead lay everywhere in piles of bodies. It seemed inhuman to Lou Princezzi somehow. All this slaughter—why? *Why?*

There was a reason, of course.

Its name was Adolf Hitler.

Adolf Hitler had set out to conquer the world. And his world had risen up, refusing to be conquered. It was that simple.

To one side of him Joe Sullivan was scraping his jaw on his rifle butt. His jaw itched. When the itching stopped, he snuggled his carbine a little closer and began to fire it at the line of Germans that came toward them.

The whole damn world seemed filled with krauts. Krauts who obeyed their commanders like dumb beasts, moving forward when the word was passed, trying to take a little town called Bastogne.

Where was the rest of the army? Why were they the only ones here who had to fight this goddamn war?

The firing went on. And on. . . .

11

There was a lull for a time when the Germans withdrew their troops. But every man in the foxholes knew it was only a respite, an interval during which the krauts would reorganize and get ready to come at them again.

Men came running, bent over, carrying ammo. Other men ran from foxhole to foxhole to treat the wonded, or when it was necessary, to carry them back into Bastogne to a hastily organized field hospital.

The men who were unhurt stared off into space, their eyes empty of all expression, their faces haggard. They who had expected to be killed here today were still alive. They were like machines refueled by that ammo and ready to go back into operation once again, just as soon as the Germans came at them.

It was almost too much to expect of human flesh and blood. Men were never made for this purpose. Only unthinking, unfeeling machines were able to withstand this constant battering, this unending fighting. Even machines knew fatigue though.

Alan Bishop crawled from foxhole to foxhole.

"Maxie, you okay? Got enough ammo?"

"Lou, you're beat, man."

"Hell, Sarge—I'm still alive."

He looked across at Joe Sullivan, lying there with his Irish jaw propped on his carbine. His blue eyes showed no expression as they stared off across the snow-covered ground. Alan Bishop sighed. The war was turning them all into automatons. Into machines that knew only one law: kill the enemy.

He slid back into his own foxhole where the Mohawk was waiting quietly, his black eyes fastened on the distant ground across which the Germans were to come. Alan glanced at him, realizing—not for the first time—that this business of war was akin to something deep inside the Indian.

Paul Andrews took scalps. It was something that was part and parcel of his ancestry. His forbears had taken scalps in the olden days. Scalps meant that they had met the enemy and conquered them. Well, Gawasowanee had taken a lot of scalps here in Europe. His war bag was stuffed with them.

Alan said, "Paulie, what about your scalps? How will Michelle feel about them?"

The Mohawk smiled faintly. "She doesn't know about scalps. I haven't decided yet whether or not to tell her."

Paul Andrews stiffened suddenly and Alan, seeing it, asked, "What is it?"

He had occasion to know and respect the Indian. It was Paulie who had in the past alerted the platoon to the fact that there were krauts around when nobody else had any reason to suspect them. Now with the Mohawk acting this way, he knew something was in the wind.

"They're coming," Gawasowanee whispered.

"Pass the word."

Maxie grunted in something like delight when he heard the warning. He too had reason to respect Paul Andrews and his almost uncanny ability to know when the enemy was approaching. He slid his carbine forward and waited.

There were some men who stared in bewilderment at the man who had passed that word. To their eyes there was nothing to see. Everything was as it had been. Yet they had heard about that Indian who fought with the second platoon. On the off chance that he might be right, they tensed.

The Germans came quietly, crawling along the ground. There were no tanks to herald their approach and since they were clad in the white winter outfits, they were almost invisible against the snow.

Yet here and there a face might be seen and the Americans grinned to themselves. Let them come a little closer, anticipating no resistance because of their surprise attack. A few more yards, maybe fifty feet more. . . .

It was Gawasowanee who opened fire.

He saw the white-clad men. He watched as they came crawling, crawling. There was no excitement in him, just the knowledge that he had a job to do. He eased his carbine forward, and taking a deep breath, lined up his targets.

Then his finger hit the trigger.

His carbine spat hot lead across the snowy ground. Those bullets ploughed into the Germans who were confident that nobody across the field from them knew of their approach.

Men leaped to their feet, already dying, only to collapse and fall in ungainly attitudes. Other men died as they lay on the ground, bullets in their heads. Some of the Germans twisted about, trying to retreat, but the bullets found them. For now every man in those foxholes was firing.

The attack was broken, but there was no retreat as yet. The German infantry had been told to take those foxholes, to get inside them and so break the outer perimeter of the defense forces. They kept coming.

Now they were springing to their feet and charging, some of them yelling. They only made better targets for the men in the foxholes. Their bullets were a hail of lead across that field, a hail that killed what they hit. Men collapsed, men dropped, men sprawled in death.

There was only the sound of firing and the yelling of the attackers, but it was a segment of hell itself to the men who were in that wild charge. Everywhere men were dropping. Only one or two men, here and there, were still on their feet.

And suddenly—

Fear came upon the Germans. It was inhuman, what they had been asked to do. Terror rose up inside them like gall and their wild eyes saw only the ends of the carbines and rifles protruding, as it seemed to them, from the ground itself. Those rifles and carbines were killing all their comrades.

They turned and fled as one man.

Now they died with their backs to the enemy, shot down in flight. There was no mercy in the men within those foxholes. These were the enemy. They were there to kill or be killed. So let them die!

Max Gluber shot without emotion. It was almost as though he were at target practice. Man after man dropped before his accurate fire and his eyes constantly searched the field before him for more targets at which to hurl hot lead.

In moments there were no more Germans.

Silence lay across the fields like an oppressive blanket. It seemed almost to push down on the Americans who waited, eyes scanning the ground before them, empty now of all the men who had come sliding and crawling over it, save for their dead and lifeless bodies.

Lou Princezzi drew a deep breath. Soon now the krauts would realize that men alone were not going to budge the Yanks in these pits. They would throw their tanks into the battle and those big Mark IVs would hurl their shells at them.

There were no fighting tanks, not for a foot soldier.

Still the tank-destroyers were close at hand, as were the big Sherman tanks. If the Mark IVs came lumbering to the attack, they would be met by men trained to stop them cold.

The boys in the foxhole drew deep breaths and waited. The krauts would come at them soon enough. Now was the time to relax and replenish lost energy.

A distant droning caught their attention. That sound was coming from the east, out there where the krauts were massed, ready to come at them.

The droning grew louder.

"Here comes the Luftwaffe," somebody groaned.

"Right at us! They'll bomb the hell out of us."

Bombs would break their defense perimeter. These men in the foxholes could not withstand a beating from the air. Those German planes could strafe them back and forth. They would die here without a chance to fight back.

Gawasowanee lifted his head, turning it slightly. "Listen!" he growled.

Alan Bishop listened, but heard nothing beyond the coming airplanes. He asked, "What am I listening for?"

Before he could answer he heard a deeper drone moving in from the west. Half incredulously, he stared at the Mohawk. "Can it be?"

"Lightnings," grinned Paul Andrews. "And just in time."

The weather had turned clear in the past few hours. Now the Air Force could go into action. The men in the foxholes hugged the ground and waited.

The Luftwaffe swept in, flying low.

Above them came the Lightings, flying in formation. The men on the ground saw the Lightnings begin to peel off, to hurtle downward at the German planes. Their guns began to spit.

A German plane began to smoke. It veered off to the right, trailing that smoke, and then burst into flames. An instant later there was an explosion and pieces of the plane rained down on the dead German bodies piled high on the snowy field.

The Lightnings were attacking all over the sky, driving away the enemy planes. They were firing as they dove, pulling up and circling back, always pursuing, always attacking. The men in the foxholes watched in awed delight.

"Go get 'em, boys!"

"Give 'em hell!"

"Feed it to them, feed it to them!"

Here and there a lifted fist was shaken as a voice bellowed hoarsely when another German fighter-bomber began to smoke and wobble. To the men on the ground it did not seem that those Messerschmitts held human beings: they seemed like insensate monsters.

They stared upward, forgetting all about the enemies they themselves had killed earlier. The war to them had narrowed down to the dogfights that went on overhead.

The Messerschmitts—those of them that remained in the air—turned and ran, with the Lightnings flying after them. They headed eastward and soon disappeared.

The men in the foxholes turned their eyes to the planes that had crashed. Here and there a man in a parachute was dropping earthward. Alan Bishop saw that there were two of them. The other German pilots had perished when their planes had plummeted groundward.

"Come on, Paulie," he grunted. "Let's go get 'em."

They moved away from their foxhole, running bent over. Eyes watched them, men with carbines and rifles tensed and turned to stare eastward. Would the krauts send men to save their pilots? If so, they would be met by bullets.

The first man came down about a hundred yards from where Alan and the Mohawk were running. They saw he had a Luger automatic in his hand. As his feet hit the ground, he fired at them.

Gawasowanee felt the bullet brush his shoulder. That was damn good shooting, he told himself. He halted, dropped into a crouch, and as the German hit the ground, he let go a burst from his carbine.

Those bullets caught the German in the chest. Puffs of dust rose from his uniform. The officer crumpled and lay in the midst of his parachute lines, with the parachute itself billowing over him for a moment before it collapsed and lay across his body like a shroud.

The other man saw what happened. As he landed, he screamed, "Kamerad!" and held his hands high above his head.

Alan yelled, "No, Paulie. No!"

The Indian waited, his finger on the trigger.

They watched the German free himself from the parachute lines. Then he straightened up and there was a Luger automatic in his hand.

The automatic lifted, aimed at Alan.

Gawasowanee tightened his trigger finger, but it was too late. From behind him a burst of gunfire erupted. Bullets ploughed into the German. His automatic fired, but the bullet hit the ground helplessly.

The German crumpled, dropped.

Alan Bishop was white. He realized suddenly that he would have been a dead man if somebody back there in

141

the foxholes had not fired.

Paul Andrews hesitated. He wanted those scalps, but he knew it was a damn fool thing to do, to linger here long enough to get them. As Alan whirled to run, he followed him.

They hit the foxhole side by side.

Max Gluber was grinning at them. "Never trust a kraut," he yelled.

Alan looked at him. "Was it you, Maxie?"

"Hell. I had him lined in my sight all the time. As soon as he raised that gun, he was a dead man."

"I owe you one, Maxie. I won't forget it."

"You don't owe me a thing. I figured you were about to take a prisoner. I was praying that kraut would make a move like that."

They lay there and looked eastward waiting.

The German High Command would be making its decision right about now. To attack or not to attack. This was what would be occupying their thoughts.

Bastogne was a hard nut to crack. Was it worth the loss of men and tanks to take it? True, it spanned the roadways to the west along which the Germans wanted to move, but they had bypassed Bastogne so far.

It was a matter of pride, really.

Were the krauts willing to admit they couldn't take Bastogne? It all depended on that.

The men in the foxholes waited for the answer.

Elsewhere, decisions were being made.

To the north, General Montgomery wanted to pull back, to take a stand near the Meuse River. He was being opposed by the Americans, who were always concerned with pushing forward, with attacking.

General Eisenhower, the Supreme Commander, had

ordered all his armies to converge on the Bulge where the Germans had driven deep into Belgium. From the south General Patton was pushing fast with his Third Army.

Reports were coming into Headquarters now. The Germans were being stalled. Their gasoline supplies— for their tanks—were dangerously low. Without gasoline, no tank can travel. And if a tank cannot move, it is of no use whatsoever. It becomes a sitting duck for a bazooka man or for any tank-destroyer that sees it.

No one in Bastogne knew about this, however. They were fighting for their lives and radio communication was not very good. All they knew was that the enemy was out there, waiting to sweep forward and stamp them flat with shells and men.

General McAuliffe was determined nobody was going to do any such thing to his men—or to Bastogne.

It was Christmas Eve and already the Germans were massing for the attack which was to sweep Bastogne aside. Tank motors purred. Men inspected their weapons. Their breathing made fogs in the air, but they were ready.

So were the men who would oppose them.

The Germans came in full force, their tanks growling over the snow-covered fields, followed behind by the Volksgrenadiers in their white winter uniforms. They came steadily, relentlessly, as though each man had been personally assured of victory.

2 platoon held its fire. They waited calmly, each man now had plenty of ammo, there was food in every man's belly, and only the cold and the knowledge that some of them might die this day kept them from being content.

Max Gluber was impatient. He wanted the krauts to move faster. Not until they were closer would he fire. He didn't want to waste a single round. When he shot, he wanted to kill Germans. He rested on his flat belly, his cheek cradled to his gunstock, and his eyes were hard and filled with hate.

Lou Princezzi woke from his dreamings about Maria. He sighed. It was time to forget the bride he had left behind him and to do his job, which was to kill krauts, as many as he could. The more he killed, the faster he could get back to his young wife.

He listened to the clank-clank of the approaching tanks and he prayed that the Shermans and the tank-destroyers were somewhere close at hand.

The enemy came like a slow wave, not fast but steadily, inexorably. They moved with a sense of inevitability, as though they knew that today would see them victorious. Not yet would they fire, but soon. When that fire would wipe out the few forces opposing them, then they would begin shooting.

Joe Sullivan said, "Screw you bastards."

He was not frightened by the sight of the Mark IVs and the men behind them. He had faced them before, many times. Sure, sure. One of those 88 shells might land in his foxhole, and if it did, then he wouldn't have anything to worry about anymore. But maybe one wouldn't; one hadn't so far.

Paul Andrews was eyeing those advancing columns coldly. Men like those before him had killed Michelle's mother and father, had burned their farmhouse, had taken off their livestock to eat it. He owed them for that, he owned them for Michelle.

Come on, damn you! Just a little closer!

The thought was almost like a prayer.

In a way, the silence was most nerve-racking. Only the tanks made any sound. It was as though the world waited, holding its breath. It waited for the explosion of sound that was certain to come.

A Mark IV skidded on a bit of ice, showing its side to the Americans. Instantly a tank-destroyer fired. The Mark IV tank, the Americans had learned by bitter experience, was armed so heavily in front that no shell could penetrate that armor. Only on its sides was a Mark IV vulnerable.

The shell caught the skidding tank broadside on. It penetrated the side armor and exploded. Red hell burst inside the tank and a man screamed thinly.

The scream echoed in the air, sending cold chills down the spines of both Germans and Americans. Inside that tank men such as themselves were dying, racked by bits of metal, scorched by flames. It was not a pleasant way to die. . . .

Yet the Germans came on steadily.

Alan Bishop put his finger on his carbine trigger. The krauts walking behind and beside those tanks were almost within the range he had set for them. Just a few feet more, now. . . .

The foxholes seemed to explode all at the same time. Carbine and rifle fire swept across the snowy fields. It made a hail of lead that swept away everything it touched. The Germans went down.

They fell in lines, just as they had been coming. There was no relief for them. There was nowhere to hide except behind a big Mark IV. They were here under orders to attack, to sweep away the Americans. This was their job.

But how did one do such a job when those foxholes they were to clean out kept killing them? They saw nothing to shoot at, except the business ends of the automatic weapons which were killing them.

Men cursed. Men wept in the anger that shook them. Yet they kept coming.

They had been told that it was only a token force they

faced. There weren't enough soldiers in this perimeter around Bastogne to keep them out. All they had to do was move forward and by the irresistable fury of their attack, the Americans were sure to break.

They had the Mark IV tanks with them, didn't they? Each infantryman knew what a powerful force of destruction those tanks were. The only trouble was, the tanks began to fire, but their shells went over the heads of the soldiers in those foxholes.

The tanks could not depress their 88s low enough to hit those holes in the ground. And the men in those holes shot with the uncanny marksmanship of sharpshooters.

The Germans fired, but they saw nohing at which to shoot beyond the muzzles of the automatic weapons that sprayed their ranks with hot lead. Their bullets went high beyond the foxholes. But the men in the foxholes did not shoot high.

A lieutenant screamed his fury, firing his Luger automatic as he ran forward. There must be a way to break these damned Americans! The lieutenant had fought in France. He had seen the French swept away by the power of the German arms.

He had fought in Russia, too, before Stalingrad. He knew that war was hell, as an American general had said, long ago. But nothing could withstand the German army. It has been trained to sweep away everything before it.

The only trouble was, the Americans refused to be swept away. They had dug themselves into the ground and they fought back with every weapon on which they could lay their hands.

"Forward, forward," screamed the lieutenant.

A bullet caught him in the chest, just as two more drove into his legs. He was dying as he stumbled. He was dead when he hit the ground.

Alan Bishop muttered, "Where are they getting all the men?"

He did not know it, but the Germans were committing all their power into this drive through Belgium on the gamble that they would be able to split the Allied Armies and then attack each one separately.

Hitler had foreseen that this was to be his course. He had given the orders that had committed the German might into this battle.

He had never expected to be stopped at Bastogne.

12

The Sherman tanks were fighting now, pumping their shells above the heads of the men in the foxholes, slamming them into the big Mark IVs. They maneuvered for a crack at the sides of those huge tanks. To do so they had to expose their own tanks to the firepower of the Germans.

A Sherman was hit, then another. They exploded with a sound that was worse than any clap of thunder. Men died inside those tanks, some so swiftly that they never knew what killed them.

The Sherman tanks were supported by the tank-destroyers, hurling their own shells at the Germans. The barrage of shells continued, deafening the German infrantrymen and the Americans in the foxholes.

The men in the foxholes had no way of stopping a tank. Their job was to hold back those oncoming infantrymen, to kill them where they moved. They fired until their rifle barrels were too hot to touch. They killed without mercy, without pity. It was a job they had been given and they did it to the best of their ability.

There was no rest, no respite. As long as the krauts kept coming, their job was to kill them.

Max Gluber quivered with delight as he shot. There was no pleasure in life so great as this, to be able to kill these men who had murdered his kindred, who had slaughtered six million of his people in their infamous gas ovens.

Sometimes the thought came to him that this was why

he had been created: to kill Germans. He was God's answer to Adolf Hitler. For every Jew who had paid with his life for being Jewish, so must a German also pay for having allowed such a person as Adolf Hitler to come to power.

He was supported by an inner conviction that he would not die until the Germans were a broken people. It was his skill with an automatic weapon that would help to break them. For this he had gone to America, had enlisted in its army, had trained and obeyed every command given to him.

Now he was reaping his reward.

He saw three Germans running forward. He slid his carbine sideways and triggered it, blowing away the krauts as though they were targets set up at a booth at a county fair. He shot to kill, and he killed with every shot, or so it seemed.

Max drew a deep breath, staring.

There were not so many krauts now. Most of them lay in huddled heaps on the ground, on top of the dead who had lain there since yesterday.

"Come on," he muttered. "Send me some more."

Joe Sullivan grinned through a dirt-splattered face. "Hey, Maxie. Don't you ever get tired of shooting?"

"Never. And don't interrupt my prayers."

"Prayers? What are you praying for?"

"More Germans to kill!"

Joe Sullivan shook his head. He hated the krauts himself, but his hate was a pale thing alongside the fury that shook Max Gluber. He was glad Max was on his side.

The attack began to break. Men were turning and fleeing, with bullets zipping among them to speed them on their way. Half a dozen Mark IV tanks lay smouldering, wrecked. The other tanks were turning to run, to regroup and come back again.

There was a sudden silence.

Gawasowanee turned his head to grin at Alan Bishop. "Hey, Sarge. We lived through another one."

"You know, Paulie, I've been wondering. Are we the only people in this goddamn army? Where in hell's the rest of them?"

The Mohawk chuckled. "They gave us the job of smashing the krauts, Sarge. They figured we're the best outfit in the whole army. Let us do the killing."

"I'm getting tired of it."

"Yeah, I know what you mean. They keep coming and we keep killing."

"At least we're still alive."

Paul Andrews stared out across the field at the dead bodies and the burned-out tanks. Life had to mean more than this, more than shooting and shooting and watching men die.

He thought about Michelle. By God! When he went back to her, if he ever did, he would forget all about how young she was. He would take her in his arms and drop her on a bed and let her know how much she had come to mean to him.

It was not a matter of getting his rocks off either. He meant to marry her, to take her as his wife. If God let him, he would settle down here in Belgium on her farm and rebuild it. He would make it the best goddamn farm in the whole country.

He chuckled. In a sense, he had to thank the krauts for that. If it hadn't been for them and this war, he would never have met Michelle.

"Sarge," he asked suddenly, "what are you going to do when the war's over?"

Alan Bishop looked at him. "Do? Go back to being a reporter, I suppose. Why?"

"I was just thinking. If I stay here and marry that kid, I'll run that farm she owns. I know a lot about farms, Sarge. I could make it into a good paying proposition."

"Yeah. You could do worse."

Paul muttered dreamily, "I helped build skyscrapers in New York before the war. I used to run around on those iron beams high above the ground without a care in the world. Now—well, I'm not so sure I could do that any more."

Alan shook his head. "I could never do that—run around on those beams, I mean. I'd fall off."

The Mohawk eyed his hard face a moment. "You could do worse than her aunt, you know."

Alan nodded. "I've been considering it. She'd have to come to the States though. I'd never be able to make a living here the way you could."

It's something to think about though."

Overhead clouds mottled the sky. It looked as if it might snow again. The cold was frightful and the men in the foxholes, cramped and fearful of moving about for fear of drawing enemy fire, could only wriggle and curse.

The krauts were no better off, they knew. They were huddled out there, feeling the cold just as much as were the men in the foxholes. From time to time the Americans could catch the glimmer of a fire which did nothing to ease their own discomfort. They wished they might build a fire safely.

From time to time the big guns thundered, sending their shells into Bastogne. Joe Sullivan, lying as flat to the ground as he could get, hoped and prayed that none of those shells would drop into the foxhole where he was lying.

If it did, he would be splattered over half of Belgium.

It was not a nice feeling.

Why didn't the krauts come at them again? If they did, the action would take his mind off his troubles. It would give him something to do. Anything was better than lying here, freezing to death.

He remembered one fight he had had in his early years as a boxer, when he had fought in a big barn of a place during the winter. For some reason the heat was at a minimum in that place and the cold had made him desperate. He had flung himself at his opponent in a flurry of fists and to his surprise, had landed a number of hard punches.

Joe grinned, recalling the surprised look on the face of his opponent. What had his name been? Oh, yeah. Jim Maxwell, the Tonawanda Terror.

He had knocked him out in three rounds. Joe wished that he was in the ring again with him. The dancing around, the jabbing and the punching would have stirred his blood.

He would never fight in the ring again. His career, such as it was, was at an end. Might be he would take the advice of his friends and get a job as a college coach. He would be okay at that. He knew all the moves. All he had to do was impart his hard-won knowledge to some of those college boys.

Why not? Settle down in some nice college town, buy himself a house where he could grow flowers and life would be sweet once again. If he could develop one of those college boys into championship class, for instance, then manage him to a title . . . well! That would be almost as good as if he'd won the crown himself.

To one side of him Maxie Gluber gloomed. Where in hell were the krauts anyhow? How long did it take them to regroup and come at us again? He hoped they weren't getting second thoughts. If they were, they might be abandoning the idea of taking Bastogne.

"Where are you?" he muttered. "We're here, waiting. Come on, you sons-of-bitches. *Come on!*"

Lou Princezzi slept. He was exhausted and this was as good a time as any to snatch a few minutes of slumber. He had settled himself into his hole as comfortably as possible, trying to ignore the cold that ate at him, and he had closed his eyes.

He dreamed of Maria as he usually did. Lou thought that God was either taunting him or promising him a happy future with his bride. Maybe his dreams were God's way of encouraging him, telling him to keep going.

Maria was standing in a canoe, taking her clothes off. They were all alone on a big lake. He was paddling the canoe and yelling at her to sit down. But she was lifting off her dress, showing him her legs in black stockings, the garters, the frilly black underthings she was wearing.

She was laughing at him, gently teasing. The dress swept upwards and he could see her bare breasts jiggling. Her nipples were dark, long. His mouth began to water at the sight of them and he wanted to fling himself at her.

He could not move. He could not even paddle. His arms hung at his side and he could only stare.

Marie put her palms under her breasts and lifted them toward him, shaking them a little. Just as she had often done on their honeymoon when she wanted to rouse him to a frenzy. On the honeymoon she had made him sit in a chair and not move while she did a little striptease for him. It had driven him nuts, watching her, getting hotter and hotter, seeing her taking her clothes off.

She put her thumbs in her panties and wriggled her hips, pushing down the panties. He was straining his eyes to see her black pubic bush when . . . .

His eyes opened. He was staring at the frozen ground of the foxhole, his hands gripping tightly around his rifle, his body almost contorted into a fetal position.

"Christ," he whispered.

The dream had been so vivid, it took him a moment or two until the reality had its way with him. He straightened slowly, cursing under his breath.

He lifted his head and peered above the rim of the foxhole. The Germans were still out there, far away. He could not see them, but he could make out the winking of the fireflames around which some of them were crouched.

"What are you waiting for?" he snarled. "Do you want this war to go on forever?"

In time they came, the sound of their tanks reaching them first, the clanking and the clatter. They swept forward in a wave of men and metal and the 88s were hammering shells as fast as the men in those tanks could load.

The men in the foxholes ducked instinctively.

Here and there a shell landed in a hole and the men could hear the splash and splatter of blood and flesh. But mostly the shells went overhead, landing somewhere behind them. They knew death was coming at them, but they had faced death before.

It would be their turn to throw death next. Already they could see the men of the 901st regiment of Panzer Lehr and the 26th Volksgrenadiers advancing steadily behind the oncoming tanks.

The tank-destroyers went into action. They had deployed off to the left and right, which gave them a flank position with relation to the huge Mark IVs, and they were already hammering their shells at those tanks.

One tank exploded, but the others came on.

A Mark IV zeroed in on a tank-destroyer, blasted it

with its gun. The tank-destroyer was a thing of twisted metal and flames in a few seconds.

The tanks were firing steadily, faced with the fire from the Sherman tanks. A Sherman tank was no match for a Mark IV. It didn't have enough armor on it to withstand those 88 shells. One Sherman was destroyed, then another.

The men of 2 platoon bellied down closer to the earth. This was no fight of theirs, not yet. They could do nothing against tanks. Their job was to handle to swarming troops following those metal monsters.

At least the tanks were not firing at them. They were concentrating on the Shermans and the tank-destroyers.

Max Gluber whispered, "Just a little closer. Just a littled closer."

Lou Princezzi snarled. There was the light of madness in his eyes. If it weren't for those goddamned krauts, he could be with Maria, right now, getting ready for Christmas.

Christmas! Funny, he had forgotten all about that here in these holes. When was it anyhow? Oh, yeah. Tomorrow was Christmas Eve. Seemed funny somehow to think of Christmas when he was waiting here to kill Germans.

He wondered if any of the others were thinking about Christmas right now.

He saw the Volksgrenadiers were closer. Close enough to shoot now. He eased his gun forward and put his finger to its trigger.

It was as though every man in those foxholes had the same idea. Almost in the same instant, fire burst from their guns. A hail of lead swept across the battlefield.

The Volksgrenadiers dropped in rows. They simply fell, making no sound, and they lay sprawled in the contortions of death, covering the ground. Here and there a man moved, but only for a moment.

The advancing lines seemed to halt, as though each man in those lines had had enough of that leaden hail they were being asked to face. Those Americans shot like devils out of hell. They aimed and they fired, and they hit what they aimed at. It made no difference to them that they were outmanned and outgunned.

They didn't know when to quit.

They just stuck there and fought back and waited for you to throw more bodies at them to shoot.

Something like hysteria swept the German ranks. For many days now they had been trying to overcome this pocket of resistance to the all-out drive the Fuehrer had ordered. It still stood, braced for attack, firing back like demented men.

There was no sense in it. Why didn't they surrender, as any sensible person would have done? But—oh, no. They just stiffened their backbones and went on fighting as though that was all they knew how to do.

The Germans fired at the foxholes, but they could see little at which to shoot: the tip of a helmet, the muzzle of a carbine or rifle. If any of them froze in position to take aim, they were cut down instantly.

Even if they ran, they were chopped to pieces by the hail of lead which swept from the American positions. Nothing human could stand against such shooting.

Hitler himself could not take it, were he here. No, or Baron von Manteuffel who was commanding the Germans. Let them come out here in the front lines and see how long they would be ordering an all-out attack!

Men saw their comrades mowed down seconds before lead ripped into them. There was no time for thought. All one had to do was move forward and sooner or a bit later those Americans would finish you off.

It was not to be endured!

Ha! And the tanks. A fat lot of good they were to the man on foot. Sure, sure. They knocked out a Sherman or two and smashed a couple of tank-destroyers. But they caught a few shells in doing so and then they burned. They also cooked the men alive who were trapped inside them.

It was not a nice way to die.

The Germans came on stubbornly, almost as though they were afraid to turn their backs and retreat. They fired, but their bullets did little damage. The men in the foxholes hugged the ground and made their return fire count.

They swept the fields before them with lead and anything caught in that hail lost its life. Bodies covered the ground.

Alan Bishop was filled with amazement. How could the German High Command sentence those men to death like this? They were like automatons, moving forward into the teeth of American bullets.

"The krauts don't think, except for their commanders," said a voice beside him.

Alan turned to see the haggard face of the Mohawk. He knew a vast surprise. It was almost as if the Indian had been reading his mind.

"They're crazy, the lot of them," he muttered.

"No. But they're schooled to obey. It doesn't matter what stupid bastard gives the order, they obey it." He grinned. "Us Americans aren't like that."

Alan had to laugh. They had been told to hold Bastogne and they were holding it, just as the krauts had been told to take it. We're so goddamn stubborn we won't let them have it, he found himself thinking.

"Here come some more," he murmured.

He and Gawasowanee forgot to talk in the desperate need to kill the enemy before they themselves were killed. They leveled their carbines and they fired at the oncoming, white-clad Germans until there were no more Germans to shoot at.

The tanks were fighting it out, with the American tank-destroyers moving around for a clear shot at the sides of the Mark IVs. The explosion of shells, the thunder they made as they hit the German tanks, was deafening.

A Mark IV ran out of gas. It slowed to a complete stop while it still pumped its shells, it did not move. An American tank-destroyer moved to the attack, firing. The side of the Mark IV erupted in a dull boom of shredding metal.

Men began to scream inside the tank.

The tank burst into flames.

The other tanks were moving back now. Behind them the German infantrymen were already in full retreat. They had had a bellyful of American fighting men. Nobody needed to tell them that Bastogne was just held by a skeleton force. They knew differently.

Or, if it really was being held by a skeleton force, those skeletons could fight like hell.

The Germans retreated.

In minutes, the field was empty before the foxholes, except for the bodies piled here and there and the burning tanks. Again the kraut attack had failed, broken to bits before those foxholes filled with the men from the Screaming Eagles and the Geronimos, the Tigers and Five-O-Ones.

The men in the foxholes lay where they were, wondering when the next attack would come at them.

Not before tomorrow, anyhow. Already it was starting to get dark. They could relax for a little while.

"I'm beat," somebody said.

"You're beat? Hell man, I'm sound asleep in my

head but my body goes on fighting."

"Anybody got a butt?"

"I got smokes but I got no matches."

"Hey, I got matches. Trade?"

They smoked or they lay on their backs and stared up at the darkening sky. They sought to get more comfortable and most of them wished they had dug their foxholes a little wider. But there was no standing up here and no more digging. The krauts would see and start shooting.

Better to be uncomfortable than dead.

And where was the rest of the fuckin' army, anyhow? Were they the only Americans doing any fighting? Somewhere, somehow, there had to be somebody else fighting this war.

General George Patton was moving up from the south fast, aiming to relieve Bastogne and at the same time close a big pincers around the Germans. On the maps at Headquarters it was becoming clearer.

There was a bulge into Belgium through which—and around Bastogne—the krauts were throwing everything they had. They were determined to reach the Meuse River and separate the Allied Armies.

To the north, Field Marshall Montgomery was advising a pullback much to the dismay of his American colleagues who were all for a push against the Nazis. Now that the Germans had overextended themselves, the strategy was to hammer them with everything they could throw at them.

Everywhere around Bastogne the Americans were inching forward. Now that the weather had cleared, P-47s were swooping in, discovering concentrations of German tanks, bombing them, strafing the lines of infantrymen huddled near them. Huge bombers were sliding through the high skies, dumping their bombloads.

The black smoke of their hits lay like a pall over the land.

In the foxholes the men of 2 platoon stretched wearily. Night was on them and with night, the temporary cessation of hostilities—though one could never be sure about that. They knew they were surrounded by Germans. They knew, too, that if the Germans had made a concentrated effort with all their forces, they would be swept out of existence.

What saved them was the fact that the Germans were looking beyond Bastogne toward the Meuse. To them, Bastogne was merely a setback—a temporary one—which would be dealt with as soon as they had secured their forward progress.

The krauts continued to hammer at Bastogne and its thin ring of defenders. They didn't want the boys in the foxholes to forget there was a war going on. But the main force of their attack was beyond Bastogne, to its north and south.

But for the moment in the Germanic mind, there were more important objectives than Bastogne.

And yet—

In Allied Headquarters it was believed that the krauts had blundered. Bastogne lay astride the roads into Belgium. It controlled the flow of military traffic to the west. It was like a cork in a bottle. As long as it was there, nothing could get out of the bottle.

Yet Allied Headquarters also knew that the men in Bastogne were only human. They had fought like supermen. They had held their lines and delayed the

Germans.

Now they deserved to be rescued.

General George Patton kept coming from the south. He knew the odds against him—he was facing Germany's Seventh Army and elements of the Fifth Panzer—but he moved steadily forward and his men loved him for it.

To the north General Montgomery insisted on his holding action. In the opinion of many American generals, if he had only launched an all-out attack, as Patton was doing, the Allied Armies would have the krauts in a nutcracker of men and guns.

But slowly the Third Army was moving northward and Patton was traveling with it, keeping his finger on its pulse. He wanted desperately to get to Bastogne. He admired the courage and guts of those men around Bastogne.

One way or another he intended to get to them.

The men at Bastogne slept where they could that night. In foxholes, on the streets of the town, huddled in the wreckage of houses, they forgot the war for a little time, letting their exhausted bodies refresh themselves.

They had food now and bullets. What the hell else did they need?

Alan Bishop tossed restlessly, as much as he could that is, in the confines of the foxhole he shared with Paul Andrews. He awoke from time to time, opening his eyes to stare up at the star-flecked sky. He wondered how long this fighting was going to continue.

How long was human flesh and blood able to fight on in a situation like this? He grinned wryly. As long as they were alive, that's how long. He heard the Mohawk breathing evenly beside him and for a moment he envied him.

"This is meat and drink to him, this fighting," he

muttered to himself. The Indian thrived on it.

So did Maxie Gluber. Maxie wanted to kill Germans and he sure as hell was getting his wish. The Germans kept coming and Max kept killing them. He wondered idly how Max Gluber would react to civilian life.

Alan Bishop was hungry. It seemed like forever since he had sat down to breakfast with Matilda Kubek. It seemed now that he could almost smell the fragrance of the eggs and bacon he had eaten yesterday morning.

Yesterday morning? Had it been only yesterday? It seemed like forever to him.

He shifted position and slept again.

Dawn found Joe Sullivan sniffing the air. The air was clean and cold. It stirred his appetite and he thought longingly of other meals he had eaten in the past.

This was Christmas Day, he knew. Back home his family would be decorating the big tree with tinsel and ornaments, the presents would be gathered and put beneath the tree so that they would be there for distribution.

His mother and father would be there, sleeping late after going to Midnight Mass and praying for him and his brother Johnny, who was fighting this war somewhere in the Pacific. His two sisters, both married, would be getting their kids ready for church, then setting out for his parents' house for their annual Christmas get-together.

Christmas! Ah, hell. It did a man no good to remember such things. Their memory only made him soft. He had to be hard, unmoved by such things as battle and death. Otherwise, a man never lived through them.

Lou Princezzi slept on.

Max Gluber had been awake for more than an hour, scanning the field before him, hunting for some signs that the krauts would be coming at them again. The sooner they started their attack, the happier he would be.

He leaned against his carbine and waited.

The morning grew to a dull brightness and still the Germans did not come. Eyes strained through the wintry air for their first sight of the Mark IVs and the Infantry that always trailed along after them, but the fields and the woods beyond them were still.

"They're just getting ready," Alan said to the Mohawk. "They're regrouping as they always do and they'll be coming at us later, or maybe tomorrow."

To the north they could hear the sounds of fighting, the constant shelling, the thin, piping response of rifles and carbines.

"Somebody's catching it," Joe Sullivan muttered.

Max Gluber snarled. Why did he have to be out here when he could be up there around Marvie, where the fighting was reaching its peak? He glanced up out of his foxhole over at his sergeant.

"We're in the wrong place, Sarge," he called.

Somebody yelled, "Who is that guy? Doesn't he ever get tired of shooting off his gun?"

"Relax and enjoy it," someone else bellowed. "Besides, I want to go back to sleep."

"Who in hell can sleep in this cold?"

"I can if you'd only shut up."

Gawasowanec grinned. These palefaces made good men to fight beside. They joked about their troubles, about death. They grumbled over the food they were given—when there was food to give—and they complained about everything. But by God, they knew how to fight when it came time to do it.

He relaxed and stretched as best he could.

He thought about Michelle. It was good to lie here

and let his mind dwell on her shapely body, on her big blue eyes and that long golden hair she had. He remembered the feel of her body pressed to his own, recalled the touch of her lips to his.

He could do worse than marry her and settle down here in Belgium. He would be able to turn her farm into a money-making proposition. He knew it, deep inside him. If only he lived.

The hell with Max Gluber and his continual wish to be in battle, killing krauts. Life was more than fighting. Life was a girl and a house and hard work during the day.

Still, there was this killing to be done with before he could have all that. He began to wish, like Max, that the Germans would come so he could help bring their finish to an end a little sooner.

13

There came a message into Bastogne from General George Patton. It said: "Christmas present coming up. Hold on."

They didn't really need that message, but it warmed them. At least they knew that the rest of the world was aware of their difficulties and was coming to give them a helping hand. It made a nice Christmas present, in a way.

The drone of Luftwaffe planes woke the defenders of Bastogne at three o'clock in the morning. Bleary eyes blinked against the darkness of the night, but hands went automatically to weapons worn smooth with much handling.

The clank and clatter of tanks to the west told everyone in and around Bastogne where the Germans had decided to attack. In the early dawn hours the 77th Regiment and the 115th Panzer Grenadier Regiment were on the attack. They stormed forward against the 502nd Parachute Infantry and certain forces of the 327th Glider Regiment. Reinforcements were sent to help, but the Mark IVs and the German infantry kept coming.

Battalion Headquarters was overrun and the German tanks clattered onward. Behind them came the German infantry.

The men in the foxholes grinned. They could not fight tanks, but they could sure as hell fight infantry. Their rifle and automatic weapons mowed down the oncoming Germans, killing most of them and capturing more.

The Americans fired at the Mark IVs, killing the troops hanging onto them and then the Shermans and the tank-destroyers went to work on the tanks. Their shells ripped into the soft sides of the Mark IVs, exploding in them, filling them with fire and death.

Company C, the 705th Tank Destroyer Battalion, together with bazooka fire, accounted for every tank.

South of here, close to Hemroulle, the rest of the German tanks were knocked out and their supporting infantry columns slain. Only one German tank survived this massacre and it was captured.

Seventeen German tanks had been destroyed and every infantryman with them had been slain. It was a complete victory for the Americans.

In their foxholes, ready against any attack that might be flung at them, the men of 2 platoon listened to the fighting and wondered what was happening. How soon would the krauts come at them? They were ready, whenever the German High Command decided to hit them.

Just let them come! The waiting was worse than the actual fighting. When you were shooting at enemies, there was no time for imagination to run wild. But lying here in the cold, listening to that cannonade to the west, a man got funny ideas.

Would their comrades be able to hold? Or would the krauts break through and come at them from the rear, from Bastogne itself? Only when word was flashed across the foxholes that the Germans had been smashed, did tension ease and grins lighten the worried faces.

Max Gluber said, "Hey, Sarge, can't we move out and get in on some of that? We're not doing anything just lying here."

"This is where the brass put us, Maxie. This is where we'll stay."

Joe Sullivan leaned across the ground between his foxhole and that of Lou Princezzi. "Merry Christmas, Lou," he said softly.

Lou smiled wanly, gripping his hand. "Merry Christmas, Joe."

Everywhere men were turning to one another, their hands outstretched. It was Christmas Day and even though the usual "Peace on Earth to men of good will" did not seem too appropriate considering the circumstances, the men grinned and nodded to one another.

They had fought here side by side and while many of them did not know one another—they were from scattered divisions sent here to hold back the Germans as best they could—they shared a camaraderie that nothing else could have given them but fighting side by side for their lives.

Someone had a cigarette, nursing it through everything. Now he lighted it, took a few deep puffs and then passed it to his comrades. Each man took a puff, then passed it along.

Paul Andrews said, "You know what I'd like? To get sent back to Bastogne for flapjacks. Then I could see Michelle."

"We don't move except on orders," said Alan Bishop.

Gawasowanee grinned. "Yeah, I know. But it would be nice, huh?"

Alan nodded. It would be goddamn nice. Just to see Matilda again, to put his arms around her, like a bulwark against the world. It would be very nice, indeed.

Someone growled, "You think they know we're alive back at General Headquarters?"

"They know. Patton's coming. Nothing will hold him back."

"I sure as hell hope so."

Their voices floated over the ground. Anyone who stood on that empty field before them would have thought them ghostly voices for the men themselves were invisible down in their foxholes.

But they were there waiting for the Germans to come at them. Their carbines and rifles were ready to use. They needed nothing but a little food in their bellies.

"When this fuckin' war is over," someone said, "I'm going to buy the biggest goddamn steak you ever saw and I'm going to eat it just as slowly as I can."

"I want a chocolate soda."

"There's a place in my home town that serves the best sodas a man ever drank. You come with me, when we go back. I'll even stand treat."

Max Gluber growled, "Where are they? What are they waiting for?"

"They'll come, Maxie. Don't worry. They haven't forgotten us. They're just waiting their chance."

A captain came running, bent over, to flop down beside the foxhole where Alan Bishop and the Mohawk lay. He was a big man, his face hard with purpose, and there was an automatic in his hand.

"I want a patrol, Sergeant. Pick a couple of men and let's move out."

Bishop nodded. "Come on, Paulie. Pass the word to Max and Joe—yeah, and Lou, too."

These were his most dependable men, men who had survived through the first drop, men who had fought beside him ever since Normandy. He depended on them, on their reactions, on their expertise. With those four beside him, he would have gone into hell itself.

Each man of them knew what it meant to slide over that open field ahead of them. Somebody wanted to know whether the krauts were getting ready to come at them from the east. They were to be the clay pigeons, offered as a sacrifice if need be to get that knowledge.

They moved out, crawling on their bellies through the morning mists, eyes constantly searching ahead of them for some sign of the enemy. If they saw tanks and soldiers, they were to get back to their foxholes on the double.

The ground was frozen hard. There was no cover here. None of them wore the white garments with which the Germans were equipped for this winter-time fighting. They would stand out clearly against the snow patches on the ground.

Inching steadily forward, expecting at any moment a crash of firepower aimed at them, they left the foxholes far behind and came nearer and nearer to the edge of the woods. They scarcely dared breathe. Each man had his carbine out before him, ready to fire instantly.

Yet nothing happened.

There was no sound, no telltale movement between the boles of those trees, which would have alerted them to the fact that the krauts were readying to come at them.

The captain with them was hard bitten, no youngster. He had fought Germans before, as had they. There was no trust in him, only suspicion.

When his hand waved, they halted, hugging the ground. Only when he moved that hand in a forward motion did they resume their movements.

They slid in among the trees and Alan Bishop touched the captain's sleeve, nodding at Paul Andrews.

"Let him go on ahead, sir," he whispered. "He's a Mohawk Indian. He's like a shadow in the woods. The krauts will never know he's around until he wants them to."

The captain looked surprised. "A Mohawk? I didn't notice. If he does that sort of thing, send him on. The rest of us will wait and support him with rifle fire."

Alan nodded at Gawasowanee. The Indian grinned. He went on moving between the trees, his eyes and ears alert. This was living to him. He could fight well enough from a foxhole—and did. But it was this I-spy business where he really shone.

He forgot everything but the woods around him and what was in them. He even forgot his comrades, waiting back there for him. In a sense he was not moving through a bit of wooded land here in Belgium, he was as one with his ancestors who had slipped like ghosts between the trees in the thick forests of earlier New York.

There were no little animals here, as there would be in America. There was nothing alive except himself; at least, nothing he could see; and what Gawasowanee did not see, did not exist.

He slid forward steadily.

When he had gone half a mile, he froze.

Directly in front of him was a big Tiger tank. Two Germans were sitting on it, casually smoking. Gawasowanee shrank even closer to the hard ground. He wished that he could speak German for the two men were conversing casually in that language.

The Mohawk eased off to one side, sliding past the

big Tiger. One tank did not an attack make. It might be here to spy on the men of Bastogne. Gawasonwanee wanted to know what was behind that tank.

He did not have far to go. Within another hundred yards he reached the end of the trees and saw the German Panzer outfit, tanks lined up, the white-clad German infantrymen lounging about, waiting for the word from their commanding general.

He whistled soundlessly. An attack was coming all right. Not just yet though—but certainly within the next hour or two.

He whirled and moved back the way he had come.

When he was level with the big Tiger tank, he hesitated. Ought he go back as he was, quietly and without sound, to tell the captain what he had seen? Yes, of course he should.

His hand itched. He scowled.

That tank was so near! Its turret was open to the sky and those two krauts were just sitting there smoking like ducks on the wind.

He lifted a hand grenade off its clip and pulled the pin. With an overhand motion he tossed it, arcing it high through the air. It clanked against the side of the tank and fell inside.

The two Germans, alerted by that sound, turned their heads to stare down inside the tank. An explosion and a sheet of flame lifted upward blinding them.

At the same instant, Gawasowanee sprang to his feet and fired a few bursts at those figures. He saw them stiffen and fall forward—

He turned and ran.

He would not be the only one to hear that muffled roar as the grenade exploded nor was he the only one to hear his gunfire. The Germans would know something was happening up here where the trees grew so thickly.

They would send out a patrol to investigate.

By that time Gawasowanee would be long gone.

He ran back to his comrades, waiving his arm. "Get moving! I just busted up a tank and shot a couple of its men."

As one man 2 platoon and the captain rose up and fled. They ran swiftly without thought of anything but to escape the retaliation the Germans would want to give them. But before there would be any retaliation, the krauts would have to discover what had happened.

And that would take a little time. Long enough, certainly, for them to sprint back across that open field and reach the comparative security of their foxholes.

The captain landed in the same foxhole with the Mohawk and Sergeant Bishop. The face he turned toward the Indian was filled with anger.

"What the hell did you have to alert them to us like that for?" he snarled.

"I couldn't help it, sir. I went around the Tiger and saw where their main bunch was loafing, waiting for the order to attack. I felt it would be a good idea to worry them a little."

The captain nodded slowly. He knew his men were fighters, that each one of them was filled with initiative, unlike the German soldier who obeyed orders perfectly but was trained not to think for himself but to leave the thinking for his superiors.

An American soldier acted on his own and to hell with orders. If he saw a chance to hit the enemy, he hit him with everything he could. He didn't stand around waiting for permission or an order.

The captain grinned. "Good work, soldier. I'll report back now."

He slid out of the foxhole and crawled toward headquarters.

Alan chuckled. "You either made the krauts mad or gave them something to think about. They'll be scratching their heads and wondering what happened to their soldiers and their tank."

"I couldn't resist the temptation, Sarge."

"You did right, Paulie."

The men in the foxholes got the word, passed up and down the lines by the men who called out to the five who had gone across that no-mans-land to reconnoiter. They chuckled, learning what the Indian had done, and not a man resented his action though they envied it.

It took two hours, but the Germans finally came, sweeping forward across the snowy ground in their formations as though they formed part of an irresistible force.

The Sherman tanks and the tank-destroyers had been long alerted. They swung into position and they hammered the oncoming Tiger tanks and the Mark IVs with all their firepower.

The kraut infantry followed them, running swiftly.

Max Gluber grinned. This was living, for him, watching those men run to meet the death he was waiting to hand out to them. You'd think the bastards would learn not to come at those foxholes with a frontal attack, but the German officer was arrogant. He hurled his men forward in waves, expecting to wash right over anything in their way.

He fired now, firing again and again.

Carbines and rifles were spitting death from all around him as his fellow Americans poked out just enough of their heads to aim and fire. The top of a combat helmet and the muzzle of a rifle made for poor targets at which to shoot, especially for men running at them.

Lou Princezzi was firing calmly and unemotionally.

Normally excitable because of his Italian ancestry, he had discovered long ago that a cold detachment was his best ally while firing at his enemies. His trigger finger was careful, his eye squinting along his sights was accurate.

Men dropped before his fire and lay still. It seemed to him that almost his entire life—except for his memories of Maria—had consisted of this constant shooting and killing. There was nothing except this and the hunger in his belly.

He was always hungry. His rations did little to ease the bite of that emptiness inside him. What he wouldn't give for a plate of his mother's spaghetti and meat balls with the raisins inside them.

His mouth watered even as he fired.

The Shermans and the tank-destroyers were scoring hits. Everywhere across the fields, German tanks could be seen burning. Their fire had stopped two Shermans and a tank-destroyer, but the others firing behind the foxholes were hitting their targets and exploding them.

Without the tanks to hide behind and to support them, the German infantry was helpless. They could not run fast enough to reach the foxholes before they were cut down by the accurate rifle fire of the entrenched Americans. They fell and they lay there and the Americans shot over them into the bodies of their oncoming comrades.

There was hell all across that battlefield.

Men went down screaming, shells burst everywhere, tanks exploded into flames and men screamed with agony in their throats when those flames ate at their flesh. There was no time for thought. Every man acted by instinct.

When you saw the enemy, you shot him.

The Americans could see the enemy before them, the

Germans could not. They knew they were there. They saw the rifles and the carbines firing at them, but what man could hit the end of a carbine while running forward except by sheer dumb luck?

They made targets for the men in the foxholes, targets that could scarcely be missed.

The attack foundered. The burning Mark IVs and the Tigers hid the infantrymen who crouched behind them for a time, but when they moved out from behind the protection of those blazing shells of steel, they were mowed down.

The Germans ran.

They fled from that battlefield across which they had advanced so confidently, leaving behind their dead and the wreckage of their tanks.

Max Gluber did not let them go unscathed. He kept on firing, dropping the enemy whereever he could see and aim at them. Only when they were hidden by the woods did he ease off on his trigger and then his eyes burned hate at them.

Joe Sullivan sighed and relaxed. It was over for a time and he was still alive. In a way it was miraculous. The shells those tanks had pumped at them had landed behind him for the most part—the big tanks were unable to depress their cannon far enough to get at the foxholes—and the fire from the kraut infantrymen had whizzed over his helmeted head.

But God! He was hungry!

"Hey, Sarge," he called. "doesn't this army of ours ever feed its men?"

"One five course meal coming up," jeered a voice.

"What makes you so great, Sullivan?" another man called. "If we starve, you starve. Hell, they've written us off at General Headquarters anyhow."

"Some Christmas," somebody muttered.

Every man knew he had to tighten his belt and hang on. If they had food back in Bastogne, the lucky devils who were there would eat it. Not that there was anybody back in Bastogne except the officers directing this last-ditch fight. Every manjack who could pull a trigger was fighting as hard as he could.

Up from the south the Third Army was pushing forward along the Arlon road. To take their place in the Saar, which Patton was leaving to help Bastogne, General Devers' Sixth Army moved in.

For the past four days the Third Army had been pushing as fast as lines of communication could be strung and men and tanks be moved. The 4th Armored Division was attacking from Arlon, headed straight for Bastogne. The 26th Infantry Division was headed for Wiltz, a little north of the entrapped town. His 80th Division was heading right at Ettelbruck.

The job of the 4th Armored—under Major General Hugh Gaffey—was to go right to Bastogne and to sweep everything German out of its way. In front of them all were the tanks and the tank-destroyers. The armored infantry would follow.

If any resistance should be met, the enemy should be enveloped from the sides rather than risk a front-to-front battle. It was more important at the moment to rescue the men in Bastogne than to worry bout fighting the enemy.

Patton told his corps commanders: "Drive like hell!"

While General Eisenhower was exhorting his men to take advantage of this opportunity to destroy the enemy since they had come out from behind the protection of the Siegfried Line, Patton was praying for good weather.

All he needed was a few good days, he told himself. He worried more about the weather, at the moment, than he did about the Germans. Germans he could handle, he felt; the weather was something else again.

Instead of good weather, Patton got fog and snow, but he attacked anyhow. If the men in Bastogne could fight in that miserable fog and snow, so could his Third Army.

The Third Army drove forward seven miles the first day. The opposition was something less than General Patton had expected and he was informed by men who had come over that empty space, escaping from Wiltz, that there were no krauts along the front.

Then his prayers were answered. General Patton got the clear weather he wanted. The Third Army hurtled forward. Its only problem was that the Sherman tanks began to bog down in the ground softened by the sun's rays. Here and there a bridge had to be rebuilt over a river.

But Patton drove them northward.

14

                     Word came to Sergeant Alan Bishop to move out. No more attacks were expected from the quarter they had been fighting. Instead the Germans were massing big Mark IV tanks and their infantrymen to hit at another edge of the thin perimeter of men and machines that guarded Bastogne.

Alan waved his arm and by ones and twos his platoon and other platoons of the 101st came out of the foxholes and began their march over the snowy ground. The light was pallid—winter weather—and there was a hint of more snow in the leaden sky.

"Anybody know where we're headed?"

"Sure. To shoot more krauts. What else?"

"Yeah, but where?"

"Who the hell cares where?"

Somebody began to whistle.

Lou Princezzi was remembering the lines of a poem he had read in school. "Theirs' not to reason why, theirs' but to do and die." Well, that was their job—to do and die. He thought glumly of Maria. She would never see her husband again, most likely.

Joe Sullivan plodded along, head bent, studying the feet that moved ahead of him. He was just a single unit in a damn big machine, he was thinking. If he and these other units marching with him stayed alive, they might beat the Germans yet.

Where the hell were the relief columns?

Paul Andrews walked in that toed-in manner which was the heritage of his Indian ancestors. He would have preferred to have been running for a bit of woods to the next trees, keeping hidden from any marksmen the krauts might have out there, scanning the snowy ground, hunting for Americans.

If he had been allowed to do it his way, no enemy would have seen him. But marching like this, standing erect for anybody to snap off a shot at was like inviting death. He did not want to think about death. He had too much to live for.

Max Gluber was grinning. They were moving up into position to be able to kill more Germans. That was all that mattered to him. What difference did it make which foxhole he fired out of?

Sergeant Alan Bishop moved his men where he had been told to move them, up there on the northern perimeter where the krauts were massing for an all-out effort to break through the Bastogne defenses.

If the Germans could take Bastogne, they would open up the roads to the west. They had failed to crack that tough nut so far, and this had stalled that great push toward the west which Hitler had envisioned as bringing him victory.

Embittered by their previous failures, the krauts were savagely determined to make these men in Bastogne pay the ultimate price for their stubbornness. Take Bastogne, give no quarter! Such were the orders.

The only trouble with those orders was, the Americans didn't seem to realize the part they were to play. They refused to roll over and play dead.

Instead they seemed to fight with even more savagery.

2 platoon swung into place, dropping into foxholes from which dead men had been removed, or digging new ones. They went about the business swiftly, expertly. No one knew better than they that any delay in digging those holes in the ground might mean their lives.

On the way, they had picked up K-rations and some hot soup from a truck converted into a mobile kitchen. Somewhat warmer, with some food in their bellies, they were ready for whatever the krauts might send against them.

They flopped down in their foxholes and waited. In the distance they could hear the clatter and clank of moving tanks: big Mark IVs. The Germans were coming as they always did, with the almost impregnable fronts of those huge tanks facing them.

Behind them the tank-destroyers and the Shermans had begun to maneuver, taking up positions that would let them pour firepower into them from the side.

The Germans came into view.

The big tanks were in the foreground with infantrymen hanging onto them and other infantrymen coming along behind them. It was the usual German way of attack. In the past it had succeeded admirably.

But the Americans had learned on the battlefield.

There was a little silence, except for the tank motors and the clanking of their chains, as the Germans came on. There was a suspension of all gunfire.

And then from the side two tank-destoryers opened up. Their shells hit the Mark IV tanks blowing them up. Almost at the same instant, the men in the foxholes began to shoot.

German infantrymen fell. It was as though some giant with an invisible scythe had mowed them down. They dropped and lay there, while the others advanced past them, stepping over their dead bodies.

The Mark IVs slithered around and poured a devestating fire into the woods. One tank-destroyer exploded. Another was hit, began flaming.

Ther Shermans were also firing, pouring their shells at the Mark IVs, at the oncoming infantrymen. Within moments the sound was deafening. Men could not hear except for that constant barrage of shells. They did not think except to know that these were enemies coming at them and that they must kill as many of them as they could and as fast as possible.

The Mark IVs moved on, but now from another flank unsuspected by the tank commanders, more tank-destroyers and Shermans began firing. Their shells tore through the sides of the Mark IVs, exploding and killing everyone inside them. Two Mark IVs tried to swing about, but they were hit in the same instant that they had begun to pivot.

Men came out of these tanks and the Americans in the foxholes aimed their rifles and carbines at them cutting them down.

The German attack stalled for a moment.

But it came on again with more tanks refilling the gaps left by the destroyed Mark IVs. To the men who fought so savagely against this attack, it seemed to come on an on. Ammo was getting low.

How long could it continue?

A month ago, the krauts had been on the run. Now they had turned about the attacked their tormentors in what seemed to the men of Bastogne to be overwhelming numbers. Where the hell were they getting all this strength?

Headquarters knew. Instead of retiring behind the Siegfried line, out of which it would have cost the Allies time and men to rout them, the Germans had driven forward at the command of their Fuehrer, trying to disrupt the Allies, to drive a wedge between them. Hitler hoped by this tactic to win the war.

Allied Headquarters knew by now that this was a gigantic mistake on his part. He had thrown all his power into the battle of the Bulge and it was not succeeding as he had anticipated.

A lot of credit for this delay had to go to the battered bastards of Bastogne. They had held. They had refused the Germans the roads they needed to move their armored vehicles forward. They had cost the German High Command a lot, not only in men, but in machines and in gasoline supplies.

Some of the forward German elements—among these the Fifth Panzer Army—had outrun its base of supplies. Tanks were bogging down without fuel. There was no way to get gasoline to them and now the Americans were getting in between them and counter-attacking.

To the north Field Marshal Montgomery was still recommending a holding action. To the south General Patton was coming fast to rescue Bastogne, if possible.

In Bastogne itself the men of 2 platoon were unaware of any of this. All they knew was that the krauts were coming at them with just about everything they had.

Max Gluber was in his element. He was probably the only happy American inside the Bastogne perimeter. At least he was killing Germans. He fired a burst, peered through the smoke, saw the men at whom he had aimed drop. He turned his carbine, fired again. More men fell.

He was smiling to himself. This was living. What did it matter if his belly yearned for food? He would eat again, sometime, if he lived.

Right now he had more important things to do. He kept firing, but carefully, not wasting any of his precious ammunition. Each bullet in his gun and in the clips in his pocket meant a dead kraut.

Someone to pay for the deaths of six million Jews.

He settled himself more comfortably, then began firing again. He saw a big Mark IV tank move toward him, veering suddenly. Its motors were deafening.

Max hesitated. If he remained here and if that tank rolled over his foxhole and stopped, it could fill that foxhole with deadly carbon monoxide fumes. He would die then, trapped like an animal in a box.

"The hell with that," he grunted.

He sprang to his feet and ran. The tank turned, seemed to be following him. Its cannon would not be wasted on him, even assuming the tank commander could depress his cannon enough to hit him.

The goddamn Mark IV meant to run him down.

Max slowed his run, peering back over his shoulder. He wondered if. . . .

The tank came on and Max dodged. He ran toward the big tank and his hand fumbled at his side. If he could get close enough, he would be able to fight back. The tank was gigantic now almost on top of him.

Max dodged to one side, then leaped. He landed the tank, began to climb it. His hand clawed at the turret cover. To his surprise, it lifted.

His right hand held a grenade. He pulled the pin with his teeth, then dropped it. Then he leaped off the tank and began to run.

There was a muffled explosion inside the tank, as the grenade blew up. From the foxholes there was a concerted roar of delight.

That would teach the bastards!

Max hit his foxhole, a big grin on his face. He swung his carbine around, waiting for the krauts to come at him. For a moment it seemed that the German infantry—who had seen what he had done, just as the Americans had—were all converging on his foxhole.

Kill him! Pay him back for the tank!

Max fired, went on firing. On all sides of him, the men in the foxholes added their own bullets, grimly determined that their buddy should not pay with his life for what he had done.

Hot lead skimmed across the field. It cut down the German foot soldiers, dropping them in rows. A German officer screamed something nobody in the foxholes could understand, standing and waving his arms at his men.

Gawasowanee took dead aim at him, fired.

The German officer fell.

His death seemed to be the signal for a faltering of the infantry attack. The German soldiers began to slow down, to turn and run. Their tanks were up ahead, but they had been cut off by the Shermans and the tank-destroyers, maneuvering to get to the side of those big Mark IVs.

The German attack was halted.

Those tanks that could, turned and lumbered off, followed by shells from the Shermans. Overhead the men in the foxholes could hear a sudden droning. American planes!

The planes flew over in close formation, then began peeling off, dropping to hit the retreating Germans with their guns. The men in the foxholes grinned and lay back. Apparently the rest of the world knew they existed after all.

The Germans ran faster, panic spreading through their ranks. These damned Americans didn't know when to quit. They were outnumbered, but they didn't seem to give a hoot in hell for that. All they seemed to know was to fight back and kill as many Germans as they could.

It was most discouraging.

Those American Thunderbolts seemed to fill the very

air. There were—how many of them? Nobody knew for sure, but they were everywhere, bombing the German tanks and strafing their foot soldiers.

Troops exposed to those aircraft were dead troops. They ran, but there was no place to run to, nowhere to hide. All they could do was keep running and hope for some sort of miracle to stay alive.

There was no miracle for them this day.

All over Belgium the Americans were turning on the men of the Sixth Panzer Army, the Fifth, the Seventh. Patton was coming fast, spearheaded by the 37th Tank Battalion of the 4th Armored Division. Twenty medium tanks were coming and behind them the entire Third Army.

These men saw the sky filled with C-47s as the Air Force was now dropping much-needed medical supplies and food into the Bastogne area. At least the boys in Bastogne wouldn't go hungry or have their wounded uncared for.

Meanwhile the Third Army had to get to them.

The 37th Tank Battalion, commanded by Colonel Creighton Abrams, paused for orders. But Abrams could see the C-47s moving over Bastogne and dropping their loads. He could be in Bastogne himself in a little while, if given permission to go straight ahead.

He called General Hugh Gaffey who commanded the 4th Armored. "Can I go in? Will you authorize it?"

The reply made him grin. He nodded to his officers and made a forward motion with his arm. His armored column began to roll, tanks in the lead, with half-tracks following, loaded with infantry troops.

In the lead were nine Cobra Kings—forty-ton Shermans—and they moved steadily until they came to

Assenois, a small village a few miles from Bastogne.

The Cobra Kings began firing. If there were Germans in Assenois, they had to get rid of them. To support their effort, the heavy artillery began laying their shells onto the town. Buildings flew apart, roads spurted upward in thick clouds of flying dirt and stone.

Men leaped off the tanks, firing as they ran, trying to discover the two German 88s that were firing back at them. Germans were shot as they lay in foxholes. Others were bayoneted.

The men in the 88s, seeing the heavy equipment and the American soldiers rushing at them, quickly surrendered. Concrete blockhouses were blown apart and the running figures of the fleeing Germans were mowed down.

The tanks of the 4th Armored moved forward.

Sergeant Alan Bishop stretched. Their sector was strangely quiet, though he could hear shells being pumped at the enemy from somewhere south of them. He stared off in that direction, lifting his head clear of the foxhole where he lay.

"Don't be a damn fool Sarge," Paul Andrews growled.

Alan grinned. "Hell, there's nothing out here. You know what I think? The krauts have had enough of us."

Max Gluber had been searching the fields and the woods in front of his foxhole. To his utter disgust, he felt that his sergeant was right. He slid around in his foxhole, trying to get into a more comfortable position.

"I think you're right, Sarge," he called.

Other heads poked up from the hard ground, eyes quickly taking in the terrain. There might be a few German sharpshooters out there though. It didn't pay to take any chances.

Joe Sullivan crawled out of his foxhole and stood. He put his hands to his mouth and bellowed, "Here I am, you guys. You want to start something—start shooting."

There was no answer. Sullivan looked vaguely disappointed and Max Gluber was morose.

"It's no use," Max grumbled. "They've drawn back a long way. I think they've busted their guts against us."

Lou Princezzi closed his eyes and whispered a prayer to the Virgin Mary. If what they boys said was true, maybe there wouldn't be any more fighting for a time. He hoped so devoutly.

Gawasowanee stirred, saying, "You want me to take a look, Sarge?"

"What for? Haven't you had enough of this fighting?"

The Indian grinned. "Yeah, You might say that."

"Then relax for Chrissakes. Enjoy the silence."

All around them men grinned. They really were enjoying the mild silence. Of course, those guns were still booming over there toward Assenois, but that was just the krauts probably, trying to force a way through the thin lines of defenders.

They did not know it, these exhausted men, but their American fellow soldiers were hammering the Germans all over the Bulge. Some miles from the Meuse River, where the second Panzer Division had penetrated, the 2nd Armored Division was fighting tooth and nail against the Panzer Lehr Division. Then the rocket-firing British Typhoons came rolling forward, adding their firepower. The German Panthers and Tigers were being destroyed as fast as they came rolling forward.

The 9th Panzer Division, knowing the plight of their comrades, were coming to help their fellow Germans. They came on, only to run into a devastating hail of shells themselves.

The battle lasted three days. At its end, victory was total for the Americans. They took over a thousand prisoners, killed close to three thousand. It was, as General Harmon wrote, "a great slaughter."

Everywhere the German attack was being blunted.

An air strike was made at St. Vith by hundreds of Lancasters and Halifaxes. They dumped their bombs and St. Vith literally blew apart and a column of fire rose upward from it for hundreds of feet.

Meanwhile General Patton's tanks came from Assenois. They had routed the Germans. There was nothing before them, it seemed. Then they saw the foxholes.

The tanks stopped. Their commander called out, but got no reply. He shouted again.

Heads peered up warily.

"This is the 4th Armored," the commander bellowed.

A man crawled out of his foxhole and advanced to meet him. A grin that split his face told of his stunned delight.

"We're the 101st Airborne," he called. "The battered bastards."

The commander leaned down to shake his head.

After that the tanks rolled on into Bastogne.

15

The word spread like wildfire in an alfalfa patch. Patton was here! The Third Army had come up from the south like a maddened whirlwind, scattering the krauts before it.

But the men in the foxholes did not move out of them. Those foxholes were places of safety for them. They had remained here against any number of German attacks. They knew every inch of the holes and to them, they meant safety.

It was not until a lieutenant came running up to them, grinning, "Pull back, pull back to the town. You guys are getting a rest," that they realized they might be finished fighting.

Alan Bishop crawled out of his hole. His face was taut. Tiredness was a living thing inside him. A few glances told him that the rest of his men were in the same boat he was: every manjack of them was dead tired.

They began their walk, moving steadily along the frozen ground. Most of them were only thinking how hungry they were; C rations were never intended to supplant regular food for such a long period of time. Had the columns that had moved into Bastogne from the Third Army brought any food? Had the C-47s that had parachuted in ammo, bandages and medicines?

Somebody said, "Man, could I use a steak right now."

"Or turkey, with giblet dressing."

"Shut up, you guys. You're driving me nuts."

The town was in ruins. German artillery and bombs from the Luftwaffe had seen to that. Yet as 2 platoon moved in they saw that the civilians were not as downhearted as might be imagined. There were smiles and grins all over the place.

"They'll pull us back to rest, won't they, Sarge?" asked Lou Princezzi.

"What for?" growled Max Gluber.

"For Christssake, Maxie! Forget about killing Germans. Let somebody else do it for a change."

Alan Bishop said, "Yes, Lou. I think even the brass will figure that we've had a bellyful. They'll pull us back, the whole damn lot of us—those who are left alive anyhow."

Gawasowanee said softly, "I have to see Michelle. I can't go out of here without talking to her."

If he didn't get that chance to tell her he would be back, she might lose faith in him. It mattered a lot to him that she not lose that faith. He was coming back to her when he could. He was going to marry her and run that farm and make it into the best goddamn farm in Belgium.

He only hoped it could work out that way.

They moved into Bastogne, seeing elements of the Third Army here and there. They waved at them and laughed, shouting out that they'd only missed Patton's prediction by a day, and what was a day in this war. It was as though a great weight had been lifted from all of them.

Mobile kitchens had been set up to feed the men coming in from the foxholes. Already they could smell the hot food and their mouths began to water.

"This war isn't over by a long shot, you men," Alan called. "We'll eat and then we'll probably get orders to get back to where we were."

"Have a heart, Sarge," somebody moaned.

Alan Bishop didn't think they would be sent back to those foxholes. Now that the 4th Armored had opened up a corridor to the south, he would guess that the 101st would be sent far back behind the lines to recuperate.

They had been sent to Bastogne to rest before the krauts had opened up what Adolf Hitler called "Watch on the Rhine." They had been tired then; now they were exhausted. Exhausted men do not fight as well as fresh troops.

No, they would be sent back, he was positive. Troop carriers would be brought up and those men who had fought so long at Bastogne would get into them and be driven west and out of the way of the fighting.

Of course, this all depended on orders.

Paul Andrews stayed close to Alan Bishop, nudging him occasionally, whispering into his ear. "Find out what they're going to do with us, Sarge. Ask somebody."

Alan was just as anxious as the Mohawk. When he saw a lieutenant colonel, he moved close to him, saluting.

"Any news, sir? Are we going back into the foxholes, do you know?"

The lieutenant colonel had fought with the men in the foxholes. His uniform was cut here and there where bullets had torn through it, just missing his flesh. He was gaunt and tired, but there was amusement in his eyes.

"You anxious to get back there, Sergeant?" he asked.

Alan grinned. "Not exactly, sir. But we've made friends in town and if we're to be pulled back, we'd like to say our goodbyes."

"I think you have time for that. Nobody knows for sure just when you boys will be yanked back. Not for a while, anyhow."

"Thank you, sir."

Alan caught Paul's eye and they moved off together, leaving word with Joe Sullivan as to where they had gone. The Kubek house was not far, just down another street and two blocks over.

The house had not been hit by bombs, nor had any around it. When they were about thirty feet away, they broke into runs, and it was the Mohawk who pounded on the door with his fist.

The door was flung open. Michelle stood there, her eyes big. There was startled wonder on her face, then delight. She gave a cry and hurtled forward into the Mohawk's arms.

He closed those arms around her and held her trembling against him. It seemed to him in this moment that this was what he had been fighting for all along. But by God, it was worth it, all those hours of firing, or freezing, of not knowing from one minute to the next whether you would live out the day.

He kissed her, not as though she were a child, but as though she were the one woman in the world for him. Michelle kissed him back, pressing herself into him.

Alan Bishop brushed past them, not even glancing at them. He wanted to find Matilda, to tell her he was safe and that he would come back to her when he could. He had thought a lot about Matilda Kubek while in that foxhole fighting for his life. He had come to a decision.

She was in the kitchen, staring down into a big soup kettle. As she heard his footstep, she turned, and her eyes widened.

"Alan! You are safe."

She dropped the long-handled spoon she had been holding at what she read in his eyes and took a step toward him. He came to meet her, closing his arms around her, reaching with his lips for hers.

They kissed open-mouthed, clinging and trembling a little. His hands went up and down her back, as though to reassure himself that this was actually happening, that he held her and that they were both alive.

When they drew away, she whispered, "You're still alive! It is incredible. Michelle and I have been praying ever since you left here. And—and Paul? Is he well?"

Alan grinned. "He's kissing Michelle right now in the front doorway."

She laughed. "Ha! Once I would have cuffed her ears for such a thing. But now—I think all the rules are nonsense in a way. Just so long as they are happy."

He still held her pressed against him. He could feel the curve of her belly and the shape of her thighs. She was an exciting woman, this one. A woman he would like to call his wife. He had never met anyone who affected him so strongly. No, not even Madge Thomas.

"Never mind them," he said slowly.

She stared up into his eyes, even as her mouth slowly widened into a smile. "Eh? So you don't want to talk about your buddy and my niece? What do you want to talk about?"

"Us."

"Oh? And what about us?"

Now that he had forced the issue, what was he going to say to her? That he loved her, and wanted her for his wife? Hell! Why not?

"How would you like to come back to the United States with me when this war is over?"

Her eyebrows arched. "As your wife?"

Alan grinned. "I guess I'm not making myself clear. Of course as my wife."

Her face was radiant. "Are you sure this isn't just your loneliness talking?"

Alan shook his head. "I'm too old to be affected by loneliness." He chuckled. "I'm no kid, you know."

"And neither am I," she stated drily.

"That's why I think we can make this work between us. I'm a newspaper reporter—a good one. Just as soon as peace is declared, I'll come here, we'll get married, and then we'll go to the States."

She smiled and pressed against him. "I would like that, Alan. More than I can say."

"Then it's settled. Now I'd better go collect Paul and return to our platoon. We'll be going out pretty soon, I think. To another—rest area."

"You must go so soon?"

"I think we'd better. If we're to be moved out, I'll want to be with my boys."

She nodded soberly, then brightened. "But surely you can stay long enough for a piece of cake and some coffee?" She made a face. "The coffee is weak, I know, but it is still coffee."

Alan hesitated, then shrugged his shoulders. He and his platoon had been fighting for days on end here at Bastogne. They needed rest and relaxation. But what better way to get it, for him and the Mohawk, than to enjoy some talk with these women they loved and to munch on homemade cake?

"We'll stay," he grinned.

Gawasowanee pushed Michelle back a little from him as he stepped through the doorway and closed the door behind him. He was tired, just about exhausted, but the sight of Michelle's pretty young face turned up to him made pleasure run like a torrent through his veins.

He said slowly, "You'll be all right, now. The Third Army has made contact with us. It's opened a corridor so we can get out."

She said nothing, only stared up at him with those big

blue eyes. It was as though she waited to hear him say something.

Paul Andrews drew a deep breath.

"If you'll have me, we can get married just as soon as the war's over. Then I'll be free to come back here and spend the rest of my life with you."

Her lips quivered, her eyes filled with tears. Paul Andrews thought he had never seen anyone so beautiful. He ached to take her in his arms; if she had been older, he would have done so—and to hell with the rest of the world.

But she was still only a child.

We-ell, not a child, exactly. His body was remembering the imprint of her body as it had fitted itself to his so naturally when she had opened the door. He had been aware of her as a woman then.

Back in the States people might frown on a marriage between a grown man and a young girl. In some parts of the States, of course, it would be perfectly normal for him to marry her. Down South, for example.

But this was Belgium. How did folks in Belgium feel about girls getting married when they were fourteen or fifteen? He did not know. He would have to find out.

There was only one way to do that. He caught Michelle and held her against him, kissing her upturned mouth.

"I guess I'd better go ask your aunt if I can marry you," he murmured.

"That would be a good idea," she said soberly, but her eyes shone with laughter.

"How long would we have to wait? Until you're eighteen?"

"Eighteen? I'd be an old lady then."

Gawasowanee smiled. "Not you. Well, come on. Let's go find out."

They walked into the kitchen, their arms about each other. Matilda Kubek was sitting at the table with Alan Bishop. She looked up as they entered. There seemed to be a happiness in her, the same sort that Michelle was exhibiting.

Paul opened his lips to speak, but Michelle forestalled him.

"Auntie, Paul wants to marry me. We've come to get your consent."

Gawasowanee was taken aback. In his world the woman waited for the man to talk. His aunt would never have spoken out so suddenly. Or—would she? His mother would have, he knew that. And he realized suddenly that there was very little difference in women the world over. What they wanted, they usually set out to get.

Matilda smiled happily. "I think that's a marvelous idea. Maybe we can make it a double wedding."

Paul grinned down at his sergeant who grinned back at him. Alan rose and thrust out his hand; Paul took it firmly, giving it a strong shake. Aunt Matilda was kissing Michelle and then rubbing at her tearing eyes.

"Sit down and have some coffee and cake," she murmured. "Then we will talk."

Alan Bishop said soberly. "You know, there's still a war going on. Nobody knows how long it will last."

Matilda glanced at him. "What is in your mind, Alan?"

"We should wait until the shooting's over. Or should we?"

Outside they could hear the distant rumble of tanks as they moved along the streets of Bastogne. There were some yells here and there, shouts of joy. To the defenders and the inhabitants of Bastogne, it seemed that the war was over indeed. But there was to be more fighting. Everyone knew that. Hitler wasn't finished yet.

Matilda said softly. "That is up to you, Alan."

His hand slapped the table. "Then we'll get married now, just as soon as we can find a priest."

Paul tightened his hand where it held that of Michelle. His eyes ate at her and she returned his look. Those eyes asked a question of her and she nodded.

"Yes, Paul. We, too. We shall be married also. Then I will be your wife, no matter what happens."

Alan muttered, "I'd like the others to be there, to see it. Maxie and Joe and Lou."

Gawasowanee grinned. "Of course. We've fought together during this whole damn war. Why shouldn't they be in on something good for a change?"

They ate the cake and drank the coffee. Then they rose and went out into the winter day.

-the end-

Epilogue

The fight for Bastogne went on, but now it was fought by the Third Army, pushing up from the south. It came so fast that the Germans were caught by surprise for Patton was spreading out his battle lines, urging them forward without delay.

Now when the Germans sent their tanks forward with the infantry, the foot soldiers jumped off the tanks as soon as the Americans opened fire and ran back toward their own lines. They had had enough of the accurate rifle power of the Amerikaners.

Always the Americans pressed on.

The Germans fought back, but the Americans were in full swing. They surged like an irresistible wave, smothering and overcoming whatever resistance they met.

The days dragged on, the fighting was bitter, savage. Hitler was determined to take Bastogne, to punish it for having stalled his "Watch on the Rhine." The Americans were not thinking especially of holding Bastogne—though they meant to do that—they were more determined to sweep forward east of that town and meet and destroy the enemy.

The battle went on. To the north, Montgomery was slowed by snow and sleet. Patton's Third Army ran headlong into an attack by General Hasso van Manteuffel. The forward progress of each was halted as they fought it out, the Germans suffering badly, just as were the Americans.

The American First Army swept in from the north. The Third Armored Division was moving toward Houffalize. The 82nd Airborne was moving so as to protect the left flank of the Third Armored.

The Germans fought hard, so savagely that they began pushing back these troops which had come against them so confidently. But then the Americans dug in. They fought back so fiercely that they slowed the Germans. The Americans were getting mad.

Patton moved toward Houffalize, driving northward.

The Germans had run into a stone wall. Their losses were enormous. Even Adolf Hitler saw that this could not go on. He authorized a retreat.

The battle of the Bulge was over except for a few mopping-up actions. Thousands of Germans were trapped in pockets, surrounded by the Americans. They surrendered.

As the Germans retreated, the Air Force swept over them now that the weather had cleared. Planes bombed and strafted those retreating columns, bringing death and terror to the men who were being slaughtered below them.

Three months later Germany surrendered.

PRIME TIME
James Kearney

LB499-2 $1.95
Novel

The book that picks up where *Network* left off ... The explosive novel of violent power struggles inside a giant television network. The United Television Network. Outside an austere glass facade ... inside a seething hot bed of ambitious men and women whose motto was "show your rivals no mercy" ... men and women who would get what they wanted at any cost. (Foil cover)

FLAME IN A HIGH WIND
Jacqueline Kidd

LB500-X $1.50
Adventure

A Powerful novel of romance and adventure on the high seas. The War of 1812 ended for all but Capt. Denny Poynter. Branded pirate, pursued by British and Americans alike, he fought and plundered his way around the world. But his reckless freedom would be soon jeopardized as his first lady, the sea, gave way to the fiery Renee.

THAT COLLISION WOMAN
Deidre Stiles

LB501-8 $1.95
Novel

Fleur Collison was known as the most beautiful and wilful woman in all England. The young Englishwoman would return to her ancestral home of Ravensweir despite the fact that it was inhabited by her former lover, now brother-in-law. She was determined to take what she wanted from the world ... and her sister.

ELENA
Emily Francis

LB502-6 $1.50
Mystery

The commune on this small Greek island lived a placid life among ancient monuments and clear blue sea until Elena came. They gave her friendship and love. She brought them death.

HOW TO DIVORCE YOUR WIFE
Forden Athearn

LB503-4 $1.95
Nonfiction

Practical advice for men from an experienced divorce lawyer, Forden Athearn on what to do before you tell your wife, how to tell your wife, family, boss, how to select a lawyer, and more!

DAY OF THE COMANCHEROS
Steven C. Lawrence

LB504-2 $1.50
Western

Slattery had witnessed the rape, murder, and pillage by the savage Comancheros but it wasn't personal until they put him on the end of a rope. No one dared stop them. Someone had to.

KILLER SEE, KILLER DO
Jonathan Wolfe

LB505-0 $1.50
Mystery

It started out as an innocent Halloween party. But innocent soon turned to bizarre when the treats stopped and a trick involving voodoo brought death to the scene. Someone was jailed and Indian detective Ben Club meant to set him free.

GUNSMOKE
Wade Hamilton

LB506-9 $1.50
Western

Ben Corcoran had become boss of Sageville range by killing anyone who tried to settle. When the quiet gambler came to town no one took notice... until he led the farmers in bloody revolt. First Time in Paperback.

THE LIFE OF KIT CARSON
John S.C. Abbott

LB474ZK $1.25
Golden West Series

Christopher "Kit" Carson was a legend to his countrymen. Trapper, trailblazer, scout, and Indian fighter, Kit Carson would become part of American history at its most exciting time—the pioneering of the wild west.

THE YOKE AND THE STAR
Tana de Gamez

LB475TK $1.95
Novel

"This tense, compassionate novel has an animal warmth and female ferocity that is very moving indeed."
—*Kirkus Review*

"Expert story-telling, excitement and suspense."
—*Publishers Weekly*

Cuba was ready to explode into bloody revolution. Hannan, the American newsman, could feel the tension in the air, in the eyes of the people in the streets and cafes. Everybody was taking sides; there could be no neutrals in the coming conflict. Hannan thought he could stay out of it. He was wrong. Love for a beautiful revolutionary pushed him past the point of no return.

THE RETURN OF JACK THE RIPPER
Mark Andrews

LB476KK $1.75
Novel

An English acting company opened a Broadway play based on the bloody Ripper murders of 1888. Just as the previews began, a prostitute was found dead in a theatre alley—disembowelled, her throat slashed. Other murders followed, and soon the city was gripped in terror. Had the most monstrous figure in the annals of crime returned to kill again?

THE RED DANIEL LB477DK $1.50
Duncan MacNeil Adventure

The Royal Strathspey's, Britain's finest regiment, are dispatched to South Africa to take command in the bloody Boer War and find the most fabulous diamond in all of South Africa—The Red Daniel.

SLAVE SHIP LB478KK $1.75
Harold Calin Adventure

This is the story of Gideon Flood, a young romantic who sets sails on a slave ship for a trip that would change his life. He witnesses the cruelty of African chieftains who sell their own for profit, the callousness of the captains who throw the weak overboard, and his own demise as he uses an African slave and then sells her.

A SPRING OF LOVE LB479KK $1.50
Celia Dale Novel

"A fascinating story."

—*The Washington Star*

"An immaculate performance . . . unsettling, and quite touching."

—*Kirkus Review*

This sweeping novel chronicles a determined young woman's search for enduring love. No matter where it took her, she followed her heart. The man with whom she linked her fortunes was said to be dangerous, but she knew there could be no one else.

TIME IS THE
SIMPLEST THING LB480DK $1.50
Clifford D. Simak Science Fiction

Millions of light years from Earth, the Telepathic Explorer found his mind possessed by an alien creature. Blaine was a man capable of projecting his mind millions of years into time and space. But that awesome alien penetrated his brain, and Blaine turned against the world . . . and himself.

A PASSION FOR HONOR   LB467KK $1.75
Louise MacKendrick   Nonfiction

Jackson Devereaux had nothing but his rifle and a powerful sense of mission when he came out of the Everglades determined never to return. They called him "swamp-trotter" and other names—but never to his face. Because to insult him was to ask for sudden death. "King Jack" built his private kingdom, sired sons and daughters, but that was only the beginning. For when a man is king there are those who seek to topple him from his throne.

PLEASURE IS OUR BUSINESS   LB468KK $1.75
Jack Sandberg   Nonfiction

This is an explosive exposé of America's fastest growing, profit-making industry, the *total* relaxation center. Sandberg investigates Manhattan's expensive sex clubs . . . establishments that cater to the needs of the "establishment" . . . bars, restaurants, music, topless and bottomless young women in a variety of decors from the decadence of the Roman Empire to the pageantry and pomp of the Indian mosque. Whether cash or charge, anything could be had for a price.

BLOODY GRASS   LB469DK $1.50
Hobe Gilmore   Western

The U.S. Cavalry was busy with booze, squaws, and officers' wives. But Redband, the crazed renegade Sioux was on the warpath and would stop at nothing to have revenge on white men . . . and white women.

TARK AND THE GOLDEN TIDE
Colum MacConnell

LB470DK $1.50
Fantasy

Usurped heir to the throne of the Tumbling Cliffs, Tark and his mentor Morned the Flea journey from the town of Sorne to the Silver Mountains transporting the coveted blue sapphire that is the fabled gem of luck for the Sornese. This is Tark's journey: past the beasts of the Burning Wood, the pirates of the Shallow Sea, and the Princess of the Silver Mountains. But there, at journey's end he must mount his giant fighting camel and meet his deadliest foe—the usurper Akor-Lut, Warmaster of the Golden Tide.

BLOOD MONEY
Aaron Fletcher

LB471DK $1.50
Western

Bounty hunter Jake Coulter is back as he scours the west for outlaws with a price on their heads. Now they would know how it felt to be a hunted animal.

THE WICKED WYNSLEYS
Alanna Knight

LB472DK $1.50
Gothic

Mab Wynsley and her young actor fiancé buy a mansion as their future home. Until the marriage she would live there accompanied by her sister . . . but soon the house of hope is smashed and she finds herself, her sister, and her future husband actors on a stage of death.

Cherry Delight
THE DEVIL TO PAY
Glen Chase

LB473DK $1.50
Adventure

Cherry Delight is sent to France to investigate a cult of devil worshippers—extortionists who murder, rape, and maim for pleasure and profit. The Devil presided over the Black Mass and orgies. But he and his disciples were in for a surprise . . . they had never seen hell until Cherry arrived.

GREEK FIRE   LB462DK $1.50
Glen Chase   Adventure

An All New Cherry Delight! Cherry Delight, now an agent of D.U.E. (Department of Unusual Events) is sent to Greece to investigate the sighting of an ex-Nazi and mythological creatures . . . and Cherry would get her man . . . or beast! A paperback original.

GENESIS IN THE DESERT   LB463DK $1.50
Harold Calin   Adventure

Number Three in the Mercenary Series finds a tough, old American merc with the Israeli Defense Forces. He has been with them since the 1948 War of Independence, fought behind enemy lines, in the Negev Desert, in the Six Day War. Now he was up against his toughest enemy—younger, fitter, more deadly—today's mercenary. When the two met, it would be a fight to the end. A paperback original.

BLOOD IN THE SKY   LB464DK $1.50
Dan Brennan   War/Adventure

"It reads like an *All Quiet* of the air."
                     —*Liverpool Evening Express*
Here is a novel about the flying aces of World War II . . . men who in a few months aged under the impact of assignments that made savage demands on the flesh and the spirit . . . men who flew out over Germany resigned to kill or be killed.

THE WHITE ROSE   LB465ZK $1.25
Alanna Knight   Gothic

Within the crumbling walls of Deveron Castle, young Candida encountered an ethereal and strangely silent woman. While touring the grounds they stumble upon an ancient and long lost painting—The White Rose. But there was something odd about the portrait . . . something strange about the face . . . and as she turned to her companion she felt unspeakable horror!

ANNA
Dagfinn Grönoset

LB458DK $1.50
Non-fiction

In her eighties, an extraordinary Norwegian woman tells of how, fifty years ago, she was sold into lifelong bondage, of her struggles to support her masters and herself in a mountain wilderness, and of her own triumphant survival as a human being. Originally published by Knopf.

ONLY ON SUNDAY
Linda DuBreuil

LB459DK $1.50
Non-fiction

Here are true stories about one small town's principal figures—the preacher with a past who deserts his wife and runs off with the parish funds, the church deacon and the pianist who carry on an affair made in heaven, and a host of others who feign morality six days a week only to sin on the seventh! A paperback original.

SATAN'S MANOR
Mark Andrews

LB460KK $1.75
Novel

The movie crew came to the decaying mansion to film its story . . . a legend filled with murder, revenge, death. The project was jinxed from the beginning with injury, accidental deaths, and strange events. But what would happen soon would be more horrifying than any special effects man could create! A paperback original.

BOUNTY HUNTER
Aaron Fletcher

LB461ZK $1.25
Western

The Bounty Hunter Series will follow the exploits of Jake Coulter, a ruthless bounty hunter determined to bring his prey in dead or alive . . . at any cost. It is a fast paced, fierce, and realistic western ablaze with all the elements that have made our *Sundance* Series an all time bestseller! A paperback original.

SEND TO: LEISURE BOOK
P.O. Box 270
Norwalk, Connecticut 06852

Please send me the following titles:

Quantity	Book Number	Price
_____	_____	_____
_____	_____	_____
_____	_____	_____
_____	_____	_____
_____	_____	_____

In the event we are out of stock on any of your selections, please list alternate titles below.

_____	_____	_____
_____	_____	_____
_____	_____	_____
_____	_____	_____

Postage/Handling _____

I enclose ...... _____

FOR U.S. ORDERS, add 35¢ per book to cover cost of postage and handling. Buy five or more copies and we will pay for shipping. Sorry no C.O.D.'s.

FOR ORDERS SENT OUTSIDE THE U.S.A.
Add $1.00 for the first book and 25¢ for each additional book. PAY BY foreign draft or money order drawn on a U.S. bank, payable in U.S. ($) dollars.

☐ Please send me a free catalog.

NAME_____
(Please print)

ADDRESS_____

CITY _____ STATE _____ ZIP _____

Allow Four Weeks for Delivery